FRANNY CLOUTIER

By Stéphanie Lapointe

T028189T

FRANNY CLOUTIER

by Stéphanie Lapointe

Illustrated by Marianne Ferrer

THE YEAR I FOLLOWED MY FATHER TO THE OTHER SIDE OF THE WORLD

Translated from the French by Ann Marie Boulanger

Arctis

To my little flower, Marguerite.
And to you, beautiful Margaux.

MARCH

i N
Y

EED
OU

Friday, March 3

Hey, Diary.
It's me, Franny.

I know, it's way too soon for me to be writing. I was only supposed to start my second diary once I got to Japan. But I need you, like, now, immediately, pronto.

EVERYTHING'S
A MESS
HERE.

By "here," I mean St. Lorette, at my new house. And by that, I mean with Leona and Sylvie. Believe it or not, I haven't been living with Lorette, Andre, and Henry for almost three weeks now.

Right.
Where should I start?

> At the beginning, Franny.
> Duh, of course. Okay, here goes.

Allow me to refresh your memory, Diary: exactly two months ago, I got the worst birthday present in history when my father hit me with the news—in the middle of a packed airport, minutes before stepping on a plane back to Asia—that he expected me to move to Japan with him. Since then, I swear I've done everything imaginable to make him understand that forcing me to follow him would be the biggest mistake of his life. But it's like he's deaf, not to mention completely blinded by his dream of "making it big."

The public announcement: tantrum—avoidance tactic 101.

"Time heals all wounds, Franny.
Trust me."

Whatever. Lamest expression in history.
Typical Dad.

My father's always been good at talking his way out of things, the way other people hide behind fancy clothes. Whenever I burst into tears on the phone, he's always got something comforting to say. Only problem is, his words are completely hollow.

12

Tonight, when my phone rang—Dad always calls at 7:25 on the nose—I decided it wasn't worth arguing anymore. After two months, I'd finally accepted the fact he wasn't going to change his mind. So why fight it?

"How are things at Sylvie and Leona's? You okay?"

"Why do you care? I'm moving out in two weeks."

"I know. But I'd understand if you're having a hard time with it. Want to talk about it?"

"Nope."

"Okay, then, maybe we could talk about Japan? You should at least know what to expect, don't you think, sweetheart?"

"Nope."

"Are you at least starting to get used to the idea?"

"Yeah. To the idea that you're ruining my life."

"Franny, cut it out. When I was your age, I resented my parents too, whenever they tried to tell me what to do. It'll get better with time, stink bug. And one day, I bet you'll even thank me for all this."

"You're completely insane."

"I'm trying to be cool here, Franny, but don't push your luck. And don't speak to your father like that."

"Why not? It's true."

"And here I thought we were good after Christmas . . . Are we still doing this? Is this really what you want?"

... SILENCE ...

"Dad, I have a layover in Vancouver, right?"

"Is that what's worrying you? The plane ride? Don't worry, sweetheart, you'll see—"

"No, Dad, at this point, I really don't give a crap about the flight. I just want you to consider the possibility that I might get off the plane in

Vancouver . . . and not get back on. And then you'll know what it feels like not to be in control of everything all the time. Bye."

I can't believe that after making me change schools and move in with a new family, after I've finally made friends and maybe even have a boyfriend (yeah, I'll get back to that later), basically after forcing me to start my ENTIRE life over in St. Lorette in less than six months, my father has the nerve to uproot me again. I'm moving in two weeks, to the other side of the world (and then some).

And there's nothing I can do about it.

I'M ON MY WAY
against my will
TO JAPAN

SUMMARY

Sixty-six days without you, Diary.

It's been 66 days since I stopped writing regularly, Diary. A long time, I know. But these past 66 days have been so intense, it's probably a good thing I waited to fill you in.

As I was saying, I've been living with Leona and Sylvie for almost three weeks now.

All because of Henry.

16

SHORT VERSION
·· OF THE STORY ··

(The long version would be filled with swear words, and Dad always says people who use foul language are ignorant, and I am NOT ignorant.)

A month ago, Henry went and told his father that he'd kissed me on the roof of the hospital. Just like that, all casual-like, between two bites of poutine. In one of those warm, fuzzy father-son moments, Henry felt the need to tell his dad the most private thing in his (our) life.

Why, you ask? I have no idea, but I'll never forgive him for ruining what we had between us.

Something like
trust.

To be honest, I think I'm even more pissed at Andre for turning around and blabbing everything to Lorette. WHAT IS HIS PROBLEM? He messed up everything. Less than 72 hours after Henry spilled his guts to his father, the damage was done. His mother knew every single detail. But that wasn't the worst part. She also managed to turn our kiss into the juiciest gossip in town. And believe me, Diary, in St. Lorette, a story like that quickly   becomes

After that, Henry and I couldn't go anywhere together without feeling dozens of pairs of eyes watching our every move. I felt like how Taylor Swift must feel when she lands in any city, anywhere in the world, desperate for a bit of peace and quiet. But I soon realized the problem wasn't a couple of 15-year-olds with a crush on each other (people in St. Lorette aren't *that* closed-minded!). What had the entire town in an uproar was the fact that those teenagers were living in the same house!

BLAH BLAHBLAH. Suddenly, everyone had an opinion on the situation. All possible outcomes of a boyfriend and a girlfriend living under the same roof were . . .

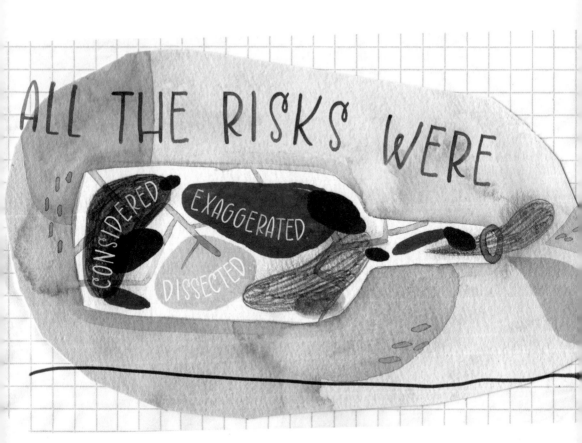

ALL THE RISKS WERE
CONSIDERED
EXAGGERATED
DISSECTED

What happened next, you ask? Lorette came to the ridiculous conclusion that if Henry and I weren't kept apart, we'd turn into some sick version of Romeo and Juliet. So, convinced we were about to flush our lives down the toilet, she decided the solution to our romantic conundrum was for me to move

FAR AWAY FROM HER SON.

So, I was shuffled off unceremoniously to live with Leona and Sylvie, who were more than happy to take me in—at least, that's what my father said. I was sad and humiliated, but also kind of relieved at being ejected from their lives (where I'd never really felt at home, to be honest). And I was sure—at the time, anyway—that the three-quarters of a mile that Lorette had wedged between me and Henry wouldn't keep us apart. I mean, if Henry loved me, like, really loved me, we'd find a way to kiss on the rooftop of every hospital in the world, whether Lorette liked it or not!

But the truth is, I've been forced to admit that Henry seems to have lost all interest in me. Like, completely and totally. And I have no clue what happened, Diary. All I know is, since the day I moved in with Leona, Henry and I have gone from being

inseparable ...to SEPARATED

Henry   me

Just like that.

BAM

... TO SEPARATED

P.S.
You must be wondering
how exactly Henry and I
became inseparable.

I'm warning you:
pay attention
because this is the last time
I'll ever tell this story.

The last time I heard from him was on February 15th, by text. I'd just sent him this perfectly normal message:

Franny

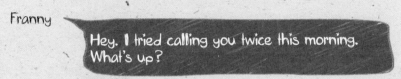

Hey. I tried calling you twice this morning. What's up?

Here's what he answered, basically:

Henry

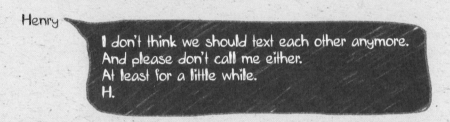

I don't think we should text each other anymore.
And please don't call me either.
At least for a little while.
H.

When I saw that (sickening) text from him, I couldn't help replying:

Franny

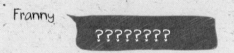

???????

And since then, nothing. Radio silence. Henry has disappeared from my life like a bad dream. I tried talking to him a couple of times—to tell him he was acting crazy—but he completely ignored me, leaving me standing there alone, with my pile of unanswered questions.

But I do still have an ounce of pride, Diary. If Henry thinks he can just dump me and I'll beg him to take me back, he's got another thing coming. I've got enough to deal with, with my dad waltzing in and out of my life whenever he feels like it.

P.S.
I'm even sadder because Albert, my ferret, is still living
at Lorette's house. Poor Albert.
But we have no choice. Leona is allergic to anything with
fur.

And besides,
a heart
is only meant to be broken.
To end up torn to shreds.

There's a reason why so many books
and movies
and songs
are written about the subject.

BUT,

I'm different.
I'll
be perfectly happy
and fulfilled living my life
all alone.

So, take that,
Henry Dubé.

24

BACKSTORY
(BASICALLY)

Henry AND me

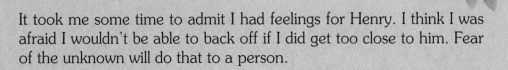

It took me some time to admit I had feelings for Henry. I think I was afraid I wouldn't be able to back off if I did get too close to him. Fear of the unknown will do that to a person.

A lot of things are scary until you actually do them. But, anyway.

Once I realized I could trust Henry, like, really trust him—and there was an exact moment when that happened—that's when we became

SO naïve.

INSEPARABLE.

January 9: because there's a beginning to everything.

It all started on January 9th, the day my father flew back to Japan, just after the Christmas holidays. Henry knew I'd be upset about my dad leaving for the second time, so he rode the bus all the way to the airport, where he stayed out of sight until my father disappeared through the customs door.

Adorable,
I must admit.

Then, as I was standing all alone in the middle of the airport, thinking something like "Okay, here we go again, Franny, back to being an orphan," I spotted him standing thirty feet away, his face partially hidden behind a huge teddy bear. I swear, Diary, I was so shocked to see him there that I looked over my shoulder to make sure he hadn't come to meet some other girl! I smiled and waited for him to walk over to me, mostly because I was paralyzed by shyness combined with a **MEGA OVERDOSE** of uncontrollable happiness.

A few seconds later, Henry was within whispering distance. I took the teddy bear from him and said something really dumb:

"You know, airport plushies are for people getting ON a plane."
"I know, but I couldn't resist. He has your eyes. I figured you'd hit it off."
"Yeah, sad eyes . . ."
"I'd have sad eyes too, if my dad were always leaving."
"I'm glad you're here."

I didn't say anything more. I hugged the sad-eyed teddy bear close to my chest but barely noticed him slip to the floor when Henry decided to press his lips . . . up against mine.

And just like that,
and for several days in a row . . .

I forgot to think about Japan,
forgot to think about my father
and about the rest of the universe.

When Henry put his arms around me that day in the airport, I got this weird feeling, Diary, like I'd always known him. And you might find this cheesy, but I don't care. I'm going to say it anyway. I even thought:

What if Henry is actually my soulmate?

The rest is pretty simple.
We spent . . .

EVERY minute of
EVERY hour of
EVERY day
together

And I have to admit we pretty much ignored everyone around us. By "everyone," I mostly mean Leona. That's right. We froze Leona out of our little trio. Cruelly, coldly. After everything she'd done for me since I'd moved to St. Lorette.

I only realized it the day I confided in her that Henry and I liked to get up at night (even on school nights) to eat cereal on the sly and talk for hours about everything and nothing. And I told her only because I wanted to know if she agreed with me, that Henry might be my soulmate. And also—okay—mostly because I wanted to know if she thought maybe, I don't know . . . that we might be ready to do more than just kiss?

I felt like it was a possibility that might turn into
more than
just a possibility,

and it was freaking me out, okay?

But I never got the chance to ask her. I'd barely got a few words out of my mouth before she snapped at me, a grossed-out look on her face:

"MY GOD! COULD YOU BE MORE CHEESY, FRANNY CLOUTIER?"

But at the time, I didn't care.
It only made me feel closer to Henry.

28

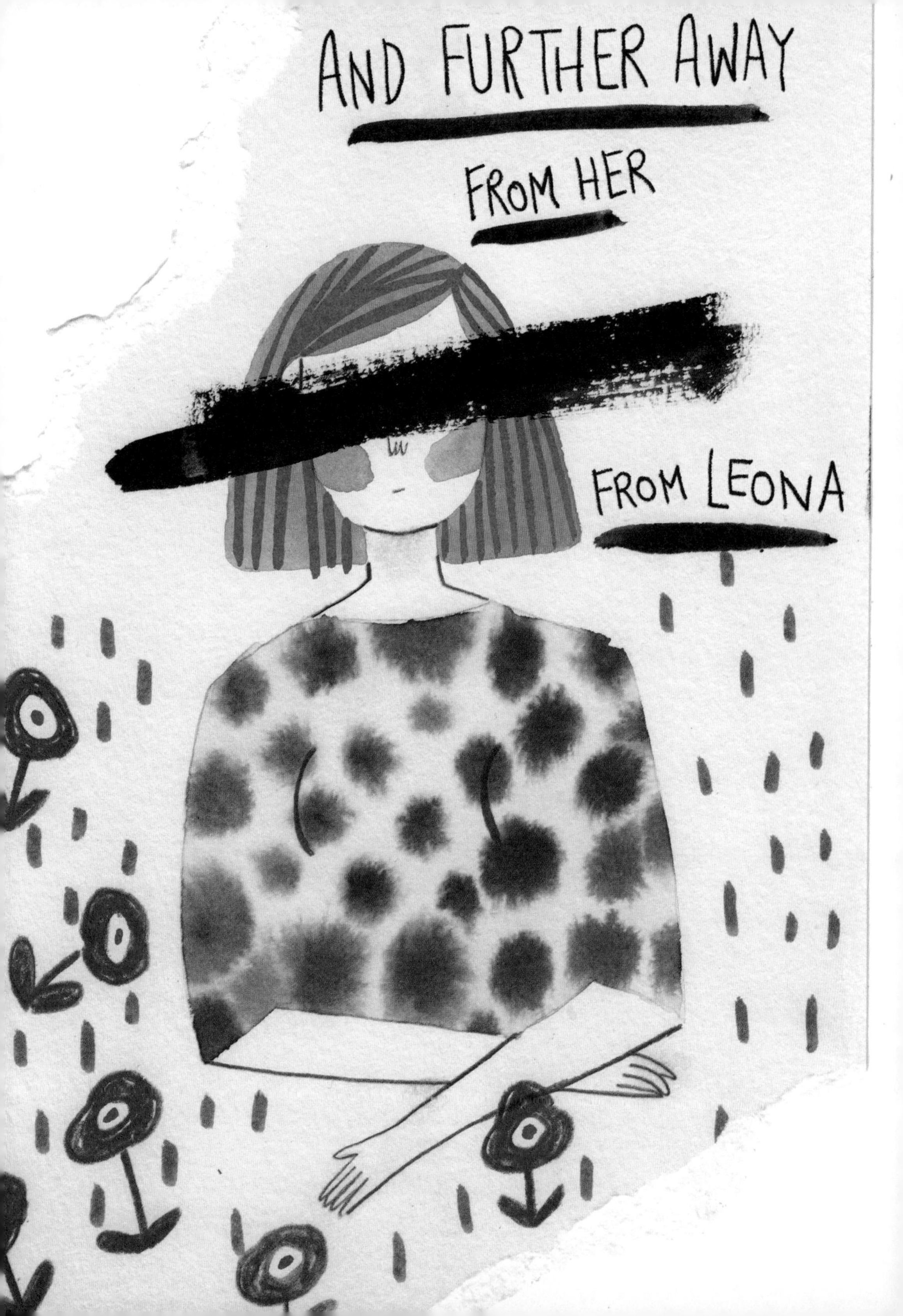
AND FURTHER AWAY
FROM HER
FROM LEONA

But everything changed
on Wednesday, February 15th.

And I don't understand
W
H
Y.

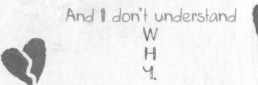

But I don't care.

It's impossible to know everything, to understand everything in life.
And I don't have one iota of energy left to spend on him.

Our love story isn't even interesting enough
for one of those sappy Hallmark movies.

I'm glad I didn't go any further with Henry.
I'm not convinced I believe that, but there you have it.

Sunday, March 5

Me, jealous of Leona?

Come to think of it, it's a good thing Sylvie and Leona agreed to take me in, because living here has turned out to be the best thing that's happened to me in a long time. The minute I got to Leona's, I felt like she'd forgiven me for turning my back on our friendship and like everything was back to normal between us. Basically, Henry may be history, but at least I haven't lost EVERYTHING.

Anyway,
living in the same house as Lorette
was a little like
trying to breathe underwater
or above the clouds.

If they don't want me anymore,
it's their loss.

Speaking of Leona, she spent all of spring break in New York, with her father. He's lived there ever since the divorce because, apparently, it's his life's ambition to make a ton of money. Meaning I was alone here with Sylvie for an ENTIRE week. And I'm a little ashamed to admit it, Diary, but you know what? I liked that Leona was gone. I mean, I liked having Sylvie all to myself and feeling, well, kind of like I had a mother too.

All week, I tried to be a better version of myself: super nice and polite and interested in everything. Essentially, I was hoping to show Sylvie how fantastic and natural it would have been to have me, Franny Cloutier, as her daughter.

33

it's a little like

breathing above
the clouds

or underwater ...

Take a look at this. So, Leona sent Sylvie a postcard from New York this week, and you'll never believe what I did. I still can't believe it myself. I stole it—before Sylvie even saw it. I just wanted her to forget about Leona for seven little sleeps. Terrible, I know.

But while we're at it,
can I tell you something else really bad,
Diary?

So, it turns out a part of me is jealous
of Leona. That's right, I'm jealous she has a mother, and
I don't. Okay? That's the truth.

But now I'm wondering . . . could coveting
someone else's happiness a little too much

ACTUALLY
BECOME
SUFFOCATING?

Did you really just write that, Franny? Leona is your best friend! What is your problem? You're a terrible person. Stop writing this minute or change the subject.

WEDNESDAY, MARCH 1, New York

Hi Mom!

I'm alive 😊

Even though the taxi drivers are crazy here, and I feel like I'm about to be mowed down every time I cross the street.

Dad took me to see The Lion King yesterday. It was amazing, but the real giraffes and hippos we saw in Africa are still cooler.

Love, Leo
xxx

STOP.
OKAY.
I'm changing
the subject.

So, as I was saying, Leo got home from *New York* tonight. And when I asked her how it was, all she said was New York is a big city full of lights and the pretzels are too salty. I think she misses her father. Anyway, I get the impression she hates New York as much as I hate Japan.

Despite everything I said earlier, I know Leona and I care about each other more than your average friends. Since we've been sharing a room, I sometimes even think we've become as close as sisters.

Something I've learned about Leona since we've been living together is that she suffers from insomnia. When something's bothering her—which is EVERY single night—she overthinks it until her brain practically turns to mush. Tonight, I was in no mood to listen to her tossing and turning. I hate to admit it, but I lost my temper pretty quickly.

"Omigod, Leo! Do you have ants in your pants?"
"Sorry, it's the jet lag."

"There's no time difference between here and New York."
"Just go to sleep, I'll be fine."

...SWISH SWISH SWISH...

(The sound of Leona rolling around in bed.)

"Leo, cut it out! I can't sleep."
"I'm sorry, but I'm freaking out! I can't believe you're leaving for Japan in two weeks and you haven't told Henry."

At that point, I let out a massive sigh because it was probably the thousandth time we'd had this same conversation, about the fact that Leona thought Henry—and the rest of the student body—had the right to know I was leaving school, town, and the country in two weeks' time.

THAT'S RIGHT:

I HAVEN'T TOLD ANYONE YET.

(Only Sylvie and Leona know. I couldn't exactly not tell them when I moved in.)

I've tried explaining to Leona that I'm waiting for the right time to tell Henry and that, besides, he's still being colder to me than a polar ice cap. But it's no use! She's been hounding me about it every single day for a month now. Seriously, she needs to learn to mind her own business. I made my father swear he'd let me tell people myself when I was ready (because that's THE LEAST he owes me) and, apparently, I.am.not.yet.ready! Why is that so hard to understand?

"I know, Leo, okay. I'll tell him tomorrow."

"Whatever. I don't believe you."

"Fine, then don't believe me. I don't care. I'm going to sleep. Stop talking to me."

silence ——————— + NO RUSTLING SOUNDS

(TOO GOOD TO BE TRUE)

"Franny . . ."

"Argh! What now?"

"How exactly are you planning to tell him? Because he's gonna be furious when he finds out you've known for two months that you're moving . . . and didn't tell him!"

"Omigod, Leona! Is he *your* boyfriend? No. So please let me handle my own problems. And if you'd let me sleep, I might actually come up with something intelligent to say to him!"

"Okay . . . chill . . . someone's in a mood. Good night."

"Sorry. I didn't mean to snap at you. Good night."

"Um, Franny . . . You realize you called him your 'boyfriend'?"

"Argghhhh. How can he be my boyfriend? We're not even talking!"

"But you said . . ."

"I'M SLEEPING!"

"Okay, okay . . ."

// P.S. //
Don't you find Leona's
a little obsessed about
me talking to Henry?

40

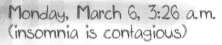

He needs to know

I can't sleep. Leona messed with my head with all her existential questions, and now I'm lying here wide awake, and guess who's sleeping peacefully right next to me?

I have to admit, even though I don't get why she's being so nosy, Leo does have a point. Henry's probably going to be really upset that I didn't tell him I'm moving to Japan. And he'd have every right to be: how could I keep such an important piece of information to myself for so long? I don't know. But maybe if he hadn't stopped talking to me all of a sudden, I would have told him!

Hmm.
Not a valid reason.
I know.

Yes, I know I could have (okay, should have) told him everything the minute he kissed me at the airport on January 9th.

> But I was afraid it would ruin everything.
> And that's the truth.
> Okay?

This silence has gone on long enough.
I need to talk to Henry. Tomorrow.
It's decided.

Franny xx

41

LIP GLOSS

MY PENCIL CASE

A PINK T-SHIRT

MY FAVORITE
HOODIE

MY RAIN BOOTS

FOR A SHOT OF COURAGE

Hunter rain boots for courage

I woke up this morning so stressed out about confronting Henry that my day was a complete disaster from the get-go.

NO. 1
I WAS LATE FOR SCHOOL.

I took so long deciding what to wear that I missed the bus.

Argh! As though a pink T-shirt, some lip gloss, and a pair of Hunter rain boots could make someone feel braver.

It was pouring out—that messy, late-winter freezing rain. Which meant I also got to school soaking wet.

A+ for effort

F FOR STYLE,
F FOR PRIDE.

That's what I get for trying to look at least somewhat cute for my talk with Henry.
Fail.

Diary, if that's happening, I must have hit rock bottom, right? Let me explain. When the bell rang at 11:23 a.m., and I realized half the day had already gone by without me finding the guts to talk to Henry, a little voice suddenly popped into my head:

"Franny, enough is enough. Stop being such a coward. There are teenagers on this planet who have been through wars, famines, and, um, deserts, okay? Things you couldn't even imagine. And all you need to do is find the courage to talk to Henry Dubé. That's it, that's all. So, what are you waiting for? Just do it."

I'm not sure where that little voice came from, but it was very insistent, so I had no choice but to listen to it. I knew Henry would be in the gym, because he always plays basketball at lunch on Mondays. So, I sat down on the bleachers, ten feet away from him, and waited. And waited some more, thinking: he's bound to notice me eventually!

There I was, watching him run back and forth and up and down the court, knowing full well he'd seen me. It was obvious from the way he kept missing all his shots. (Henry's normally good at basketball.) Tommy was there too. He walked over to me, dripping with sweat. He didn't say a word; he just stood there, sweating all over the place and staring at me with this look that screamed *What are you doing here?*

I stared back at him JUST AS HARD. Ever since he'd fallen through the ice and almost drowned, Tommy had stopped being so mean to everyone—almost like his brush with death had made him a better person. Weird. But today, it looked like "the old Tommy" was back.

"Stop looking at me like that, Tommy! I have every right to be here."
"There's no point in bugging him, Franny."
"So, what? Now you're, like, his message boy? Is that it?"
"No, just his friend."
"Whatever. That's new . . ."
"I think he was pretty clear. He doesn't want to talk to you."

I raised my voice then (just enough to make sure Henry could hear me).

"Fine. Then you can tell him I'm moving in two weeks!"

Tommy looked surprised (about time, I thought).

"Oh, yeah? Where?"
"If he wants to know, he can ask me himself."

45

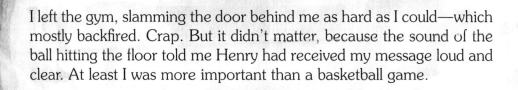

I left the gym, slamming the door behind me as hard as I could—which mostly backfired. Crap. But it didn't matter, because the sound of the ball hitting the floor told me Henry had received my message loud and clear. At least I was more important than a basketball game.

// P.S. //

My subconscious may not have been the best guide, but at least I found the guts to say what I had to say to Henry. Now the ball's in his court, so to speak.

Thursday, March 9

FASTER THAN WILDFIRE

Seventy-two hours later, the entire town of St. Lorette knew. News of my move to Japan had spread faster than wildfire, instantly turning me from "Franny Cloutier, the girl from Montreal" into:

FRANNY CLOUTIER,

FORMER RESIDENT OF St.LORETTE,

{a.k.a.}
{a.k.a.

FUTURE

Resident of Japan

I was grilled by every single one of my teachers, the principal, the supermarket cashier, and, obviously, Lorette, who always needs to know everything that's going on. I can't BELIEVE that after kicking me out of her house like an old pair of shoes, she had the nerve to call and give me the third degree!

"Franny, it's Lorette."
"Hello."
"Right. Let's not beat around the bush. Is it true, what everyone's saying?"

I was speechless. My anger was like a stopper, blocking all sound from escaping my mouth. All I could think was how overjoyed she'd be when she found out that her son and I would soon be separated by the entire Pacific Ocean. But Lorette, who always ends up getting her way, pressed on until she got exactly what she wanted.

Which is to say, the truth.

"I can't believe it. Your father would have called me! Mind you, that's just like him, to say nothing. He's going to drive me crazy one of these days!"

I swear, I couldn't help myself.

"You already are."
"What? What did you say?"
"Nothing, I said . . . yes."
"Yes, what? Yes, it's true or yes, it's not true?"
"Yes, it's true. I'm moving to Japan with him."
"For the love of God! And he didn't call me! I can't believe it."

Lorette carried on, talking into the void—blah, blah, blah—for a good five minutes. I couldn't get over how selfish she was being. God forbid she say something like "How are you doing, Franny? Are you nervous?" Something halfway kind. But, no, instead she was fixated on the fact that my father hadn't said anything—to HER.

Whatever.
I might miss St. Lorette, but I certainly won't miss her.
Stupid cow.

(Oops! Sorry, karma, I take that back.)

The only grilling I didn't mind sitting through was Henry's. That's right, Henry finally decided to talk to me.

* ~ and ~ .
IN PERSON,
.to boot *

It started with a text, at 9:48 p.m. I was in bed when my phone pinged. I knew right away it was Henry because his alert tone is the song "Shape of You" by Ed Sheeran—he installed it on my phone, and I haven't had the heart to change it yet.

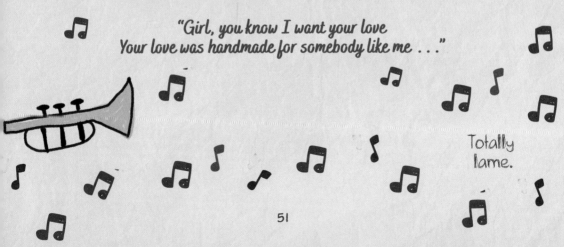

"Girl, you know I want your love
Your love was handmade for somebody like me . . ."

Totally
lame.

Even still, I bolted out of bed, snatching my phone off the dresser to see what he wanted.

Henry: Hey.

Franny: Hey.

Henry: Were you sleeping?

Franny: Nope.

Henry: I'm here.

Franny: Where?

Henry: Outside the door.

Franny: Our door?

Henry: No, the neighbor's.
Of course, your door.

Franny

I thought you didn't want to talk to me anymore.

Henry

Not by text, anyway.

Franny

I'm in my PJs.

Henry

I don't care.

Franny

I look like crap.

Henry

I don't care.

Franny

Okay . . . I'm coming.

Leona was half asleep, and I really didn't want her sticking her nose in this, so when she yawned and said,

"Who is it?"

I lied, whispering back (weirdly enough, a lie seems less serious when you whisper it),

"No one, wrong number. I'm going pee. Go back to sleep . . ."

At the front door, I took a deep breath (for courage) and stepped outside. When I saw him there, in the driveway, leaning on the hood of Sylvie's old blue Ford, I thought he seemed different from before. Like, cuter, but not exactly.

WHY IS IT,
WE SO OFTEN
NEED.....
DISTANCE

TO SEE MORE
CLEARLY?

I walked over to him, a sorry sight in my heart pajamas half tucked into a pair of clunky winter boots I'd found sitting in the hallway.

We spent at least five minutes staring at the frozen ground, without saying a word.

An eternity.

Henry finally broke the wall of silence.

"Is it true, what everyone is saying?"
"Yes."
"When are you leaving?"

"The 20th."
"The 20th of what?"
"March."
"How long have you known?"
"Not long, like . . . two weeks."
"Yeah, sure."

Henry aimed his cold, hard gaze at the cracks in the driveway.

A sudden thought occurred to me: okay, so, I may not be perfect, but I'm certainly not the only guilty one here. After all, he's the one who decided to dump me.

"But you're not even talking to me anymore! It's like I haven't even existed for the past month! You ruined everything, Henry Dubé, and you have the nerve to come here and lecture me?"
"Me? I ruined everything? I beg your pardon?"
"Yes! With your crappy text telling me to stop calling and texting you!"
"The only crappy text, as you call it, is the one YOU sent me on Valentine's Day, Franny."
"What on EARTH are you talking about?"
"Seriously? Are you kidding me?"

Henry reached into his jeans pocket for his cell phone and scrolled through a text thread from February 14th. As I stood there, reading the texts supposedly sent from MY phone, all I could think was

I'M HALLUCINATING

57

TEXT THREAD
···· ♥ FROM FEBRUARY 14TH ♥ ·······

Henry

> Whatcha doing, sad eyes?

Franny

> I'm reading.

Henry

> Happy Valentine's Day, sad eyes.

Franny

> Stop calling me that.

Henry

> Okay. Is something wrong?

Franny

> Yeah. I guess so. I think I need some time.

Henry

> ?

Franny

> You're just a little too clingy, okay?
> I need some space, that's all.

Henry

> For real?
> I thought you liked being with me.

Franny

Maybe not so much anymore.

Henry

Okay, maybe we could try spending less time together ... I don't know ...?

Franny

OMG, it's not about less time.
I just want some space.
We're not married.

THE TEXT MESSAGES STOPPED THERE.

AND SO DID MY HEART.

My mind was racing at 100 mph, trying to figure out who could have sent those texts in my place. And how? I handed the phone back to Henry, begging him to believe me.

"I DID NOT send those messages."
"Oh no? Then who did? Wait, I know! It must have been a virus that invaded your phone and sent them without you knowing."

I didn't know what to say. And I had no alibi. I was like one of those characters in a crime thriller who's not guilty but still ends up spending the rest of their life in jail. I was caught completely off guard, Diary.

Henry shook his head.

EYES BRIMMING WITH TEARS.

60

"Please just tell me the truth. How long have you known you're moving to Japan to live with your dad? For real, Franny."

I couldn't look at him. Not because he was the first guy my age I'd ever seen cry, but because I knew I owed him the truth.

And because I knew my answer
would break us.

"I've . . . I've known since . . ."
"Well? Tell me already!"
"Since January 9th. At the airport. When you came to pick me up."
". . ."
"My dad had just finished telling me."

Henry wiped his cheeks.

His last few drops of pain,
soaked up by the cuff of his hoodie.

"Thank you."

My heart started racing. I could feel him starting to slip away from me.

"What do you mean, 'thank you'? That doesn't even mean anything."

I stopped talking and just stood there, letting him stare at me. It was like he could suddenly see through my skin, straight through to everything inside.

THE EMPTINESS

THE DARKNESS

THE MESS.

I HATED it.
I HATED it.

"Thank you, because at least now I know you're not the girl I thought you were."
"Yes, I am! I am her, I swear!"

Henry's voice was equal measures calm and angry; his eyes were swirling with a mixture of pain and rage.

"I would have never lied to you. Never dumped you by text like that, Franny! You could have just talked to me. I'm not a bad guy, I would have understood."
"I know, I know all that, but—"
"No, I don't think you do know."

Henry grabbed his backpack off the hood of the old Ford, shrugged his shoulders, and smiled the saddest smile I've ever seen in my life.

"The truth is, I really wish you could have been that girl."
"Henry, don't go. I swear I didn't send those texts."
"Good night, Franny."

Then he left. And I started crying. So hard I thought my guts might spill out onto the driveway, right there, where Henry had just turned his back on me.

But in the freezing darkness
I quickly realized that,
hollowed out or not,
I'd be far less
miserable
in my bed.

So, I went back inside.
And that's everything, Diary.
Time for bed now.

Franny

Monday, March 13

Three days
without brushing my teeth

"Here, I made you a grilled cheese."

When I opened my eyes at 6:45 a.m., the first thing I saw was Leona standing over my bed. We had school this morning, and I knew it was starting to be a lot.

A lot
of missed
school days.

When Sylvie saw the state I was in on Friday morning, she let me stay home from school; she'd said she "trusted my judgment." I wasn't too sure what she meant, but I knew one thing for sure: I couldn't stay shut up in here forever.

"I'm not hungry."
"Look. I gave your grilled cheese pickle eyes."
". . ."
"You really liked him, eh? I mean, I guess I never realized just how much you really liked Henry."

I sat up in bed, even though pickles were the last thing on earth I felt like eating.

"Franny, I . . ."

I could swear I heard Leona's voice crack.

"What?"
"I just wish I'd known sooner."
"Known what?"
"Well, that you're leaving."
"Seriously, Leo? It's not like it would have changed anything."
" . . ."
"Leo, you're really sweet, thanks for the grilled cheese and everything, but I think I need to be alone."
"Still?!"
" . . ."
"Franny, you haven't eaten a bite or gotten dressed in the past 72 hours! I really think it's enough now!"

I put the grilled cheese down on the nightstand, which Leona clearly interpreted as an act of defiance because she started to get really, really worked up.

"You're leaving in one week, Franny! ONE week! Do you realize that? In exactly seven days, you'll be completely surrounded by a mountain of sushi and people who only speak Japanese!"

I glared at Leona. With all the energy I could muster, I shot back:

"Wow, awesome! You really think that's going to make me feel better? Reminding me about the months of hell that I'm in for?! Not cool, Leona Gingras!"
"Well, it worked, didn't it?"

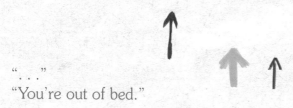

"..."

"You're out of bed."

I looked down at my feet. Leona was right. I was vertical, my toes buried deep in the bedroom carpet. I had indeed emerged from my shelter, my den of pain. Leona took a step back, like she was giving me room to collect my thoughts.

"I just think we should make the best of the time we have left."
"..."
"And seriously, Franny, who gives a crap about him!"
"About who?"
"Henry! Who gives a crap about Henry?"

I'm not sure why, Diary, but when Leona said that—"Who gives a crap about Henry?"—I burst out laughing. Leona did the same. And at that exact moment, I felt something shift inside me.

And it suddenly made me very aware of my pathetic state:

MY HUGE MOP
of hair LIMPLY
perched on top of
MY HEAD
My heart pajamas
SAGGING OFF
MY BUTT
MY EMPTY STOMACH
BEGGING ME for a scrap of FOOD.

Then I said something really dumb—but which made complete and total sense at the time:

"Leo."
"What?"
"I need to brush my teeth. It's been three days."
" . . . "

Leona stared at me for three whole seconds. Then she started giggling and couldn't stop. I think she even fell over on the bed. She'd been braced for anything—anything except a comment about my personal hygiene.

And you want to know the weirdest thing, Diary? At that exact moment, I think I could have asked Leona for anything, for example:

"Leo,
I need to go for an elephant ride,
like, right now,
please."

And I know she would have answered:

My best friend was right there, by my side, to help me get up and out of those revolting pajamas once and for all.

And that's exactly what I did.
I got up.

And you know what I thought, Diary, at that precise moment?
I thought . . .

Friendship
just may be the safest refuge in the world,
when you think about it.

To be completely and totally honest, I still haven't 100% cleansed the pain from my soul, but I have exorcised it from my body. At least, just enough to decide I wasn't going to spend the rest of the week in bed.

So.

71

ONE SHOWER,
one grilled cheese
and 3 shots of
MOUTHWASH
later...

I went to join
Leona and Sylvie in the kitchen.

After my long bout of wallowing, the sunlight was nearly blinding. But Sylvie acted like everything was normal, saying only, with the kindest smile in the world:

"I knew our Franny wouldn't spend the rest of her life holed up in her bedroom."

In typical Sylvie fashion—always keeping you on your toes—she placed both hands on her hips, like a president who's just made a decision of national importance, and said to me:

"You've already missed a day of school. What's one more?"

Leona looked at her mother and

LIT UP
LIKE A CHRISTMAS TREE !

"No fair! I want to stay home too, Mom! I haven't missed a single day this year!"

Sylvie turned to Leo with a very, very serious look on her face, as if to say *This is your mother talking.*

"If you didn't have a 94% average, it would be out of the question, Leona. You know that, right?"
"Yesssss, Mom. I know."
"Okay, then, it's decided! Now, who wants to taste my magical happiness cure?"

Yup, I admit it, we answered her in sync like a couple of five-year-old girls. Sylvie threw open the pantry doors, took out an enormous bag of flour and set it down on the kitchen island. Then she turned to us and said:

"Girls, the three of us are going to spend all day, right here in this kitchen, doing *il dolce far niente*. Now go put your PJs back on. I'll call my boss and your principal, then I'll explain everything!"

il dolce far niente

THE SWEETNESS
OF DOING
NOTHING

AND

OF THE AMAZING DAY I SPENT WITH SYLVIE AND LEONA.

When we got back (Leona in PJs and me in overalls—the thought of spending one more minute in the same clothes I'd worn all weekend was just too much to bear), Sylvie beckoned us over to the huge map of the world hanging on the back wall of the kitchen.

I thought to myself . . . Weird. That map has been there this whole time and I've never noticed it.

Sylvie explained that every time she visits a new country, she sticks a pushpin in the map—for posterity, I suppose. She placed her finger on Italy and turned toward us.

"Want to hear one of my travel stories? You'll see, it has to do with our plans for today."

OUR RAPT SILENCE SPOKE FOR ITSELF:

Sylvie obliged.

"I was 21 years old the first time I went to Italy—with your mother, Franny. Marianne and I spent our entire life savings to go sailing, right here, in Santa Maria di Leuca, on the Adriatic Sea. All because your mom had read a *Reader's Digest* article about how it had the tallest lighthouse in Europe! I never quite understood the appeal, but I followed her anyway."

I felt a lump in my throat. Why can't my father ever tell me stories the way Sylvie talks about my mother?

"You really loved her, eh? My mom?"
"Like a sister."

Leona and I looked at each other, obviously both wondering if there was even the slightest chance we might eventually feel that way about each other.

"Go on, Sylvie!"
"So, one night, Marianne and I were stretched out on the deck of our boat. We loved to lie quietly, side by side, staring up at the sky, even though Marianne wasn't very big on stargazing. She preferred to spend her evenings with her nose stuck in a tiny Italian dictionary, because she loved the sound of it so much—Italian, I mean. So, at one point this feeling came over me like something momentous had just happened. Marianne hadn't moved a muscle, but I could tell she'd just stumbled upon a treasure. She raised her head and said to me: 'Sylvie, I've just found the most beautiful expression in the world.'"

I looked at Sylvie, certain I knew what my mother had found.

"*Il dolce far niente*, right?"
"Yup, that's right."
"Okay, Mom, but what does it mean, this *dolce*-whatever?"
"It's Italian for *the sweetness of doing nothing*."
"Seriously, Mom? Doing nothing? Don't try to act all cool, okay. Aren't you always nagging me to study and work and study some more?"
"Of course, sweetheart, I'm not saying work isn't important. But the Italians invented the expression to remind themselves that it's also important to slow down, to savor the moment, to really see things—see them with their heart. And if you ask me, when times are tough and

things just don't make sense, seeing the world through that lens can bring you a lot of strength."

Hearing that, I thought back on the past few days.

"Times . . . kind of like the week I just had, right?"
"Yes, that's right. Anyway, it's my own personal cure. And it really works!"

Sylvie stepped away from the map, almost like she was saying goodbye to a loved one. Then she turned to us and said, in a wacky Italian accent:

"So, datsa exactly what we a gonna do today! We a gonna make a . . . da real paaaasta Italiana!"

So, there you go.
That's how Leona and I were first introduced to il dolce far niente, spending the day making homemade pasta!

THERE WERE EGGS AND FLOUR... EVERYWHERE!

And I'm pretty sure it even smelled like tomato sauce all the way out in the frozen garden.

By the time the sun went down, we'd already done the dishes and laughed more in eight hours than I had in the entire year before. We settled in to watch the latest chick flick with our huge plates of homemade fettuccine smothered in mountains of parmesan cheese.
But all three of us ended up falling asleep, tangled together on the sofa. Ten hours later, we woke up to Leona burrowing out from beneath the covers.

"Mom . . ."
"What?"
"If I promise to get a 96% average for the rest of my life, can we have another *il dolce far niente* day today?"
"Forget about it!"
"Okay . . . But can I have fettucine for breakfast?"
"That's enough, lazy bones! Get up! You too, Franny! You both have exactly three minutes to get dressed."

And just like that, over three plates of homemade pasta at 7:35 this morning, our peaceful little interlude came to an end . . . And I heard a small voice inside me say: "I hope you made the most of it, Franny, because there's a storm brewing."

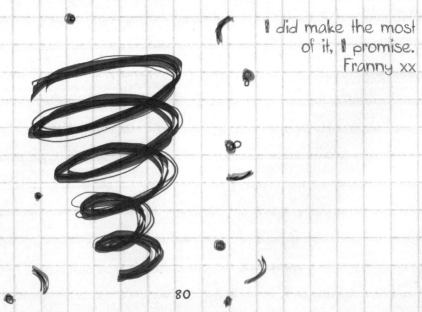

I did make the most
of it, I promise.
Franny xx

P. S. #1
The fact that I've snapped out of my funk won't stop me
from proving to Henry, sooner or later,
that I wasn't the one who sent him all those text messages.
I know someone was trying to come between us.
I know it deep in my heart.
It won't fix anything because soon we'll be
thousands of miles apart.
But at least he'll know.

P. S. #2
Diary, I'm going to stick you in a drawer for a few days now,
okay?
Only six more sleeps until I leave for Japan,
and I don't really want to
spend them overthinking, you know?
But I promise, you're coming with me.

Can silence sometimes be worth a thousand promises?

This morning, the empty parking lot at the St. Lorette shopping mall looked even emptier than usual. I was waiting for the bus that would take me to the airport when I saw her arrive.

"What are you doing here, Leona? It's a school day."
"*Il dolce far niente.*"

I laughed, but only half-heartedly, through my sadness.

"I don't think you really get the concept . . . I guess we'll have to go to Italy."
"I just didn't want you to have to wait for the bus all alone."
"I'm going to miss you."

Leona hugged me tight. It made me think of Henry—and how I wished he were there to hug me too. I think I even gazed off into the distance, just in case.

But he wasn't
there.

"I'm sure you'll do all kinds of cool things over there, and you'll forget all about me."
"The only person I want to forget about is Henry."
"I know."
"Hey, Leona . . ."
"What?"
"Well, I know you're allergic to him, but . . . do you think you could visit Albert once in a while?"
"Wait, what? You're not taking him with you?"
"No. I wanted to, but my father said he'd have to spend 40 days in a cage at Japanese customs before they'd release him. Knowing him, he'd just shrivel up and die."
"So, you left him with Henry . . ."
"Yeah."
"Omigod, poor you. Of course I'll visit him."

I didn't think I'd do it, I mean, I wasn't planning to, but I did it anyway. I opened up my bag, looked Leona straight in the eyes and handed her an envelope.

"Leo, can I trust you? Like, really, really trust you?"
" . . . "
"Could you give this to Henry, please. Like, as soon as possible."
"What is it?"
"It's too long to explain. Just . . . give it to him, okay?"
"Are you sure writing to him is a good idea?"

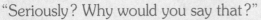

"Seriously? Why would you say that?"
"I don't know, maybe because things always come out sounding sadder and more real in letters."
"Can you please just give it to him?"

Leona took the envelope without a word. Just then, the bus pulled up, and I thought to myself, if a picture is worth a thousand words, maybe silence is worth a thousand promises.

"Take care, Franny."
"Thanks. You too. And stop crying. I'm not moving to another planet."
"You might as well be."
"Yeah, I know."
"Bye."
"Bye."

I'VE OFFICIALLY LEFT ST. LORETTE

Leona is the last person I said goodbye to. It's official now.

I've only been in the air for twenty minutes, but I have this weird feeling like, even though my body is on the plane, my spirit is still stuck somewhere on the ground, lingering in all the places in St. Lorette that I've been to in the past few months.

You might think this is crazy, Diary, but I don't even know how long I'll be in Japan. I don't know whether I'll be going to school there. I don't even know if I'll ever see St. Lorette again! The truth is, I don't know ANYTHING about the months ahead, and the only person I have to blame for that is myself.

Every time my father brought up the subject, every time he asked me if I was finally ready to talk about it, to ask him any questions I might have, I refused to listen. There's a word for how I acted; it's called *denial*. And as I'm writing this, I'm forced to admit that the 24,000 feet between me and the ground are very real and that it's too late to turn back now.

F.

xx

BUT

I'M GOING TO MAKE A SOLEMN VOW HERE, DIARY.

IF, IN EXACTLY FOUR WEEKS, I'M NOT HAPPY
WITH A CAPITAL H,
IT'S BACK TO ST. LORETTE FOR ME.

*** 4 WEEKS ***

Plenty of time to prove to my
father that he was
WRONG
to uproot me for the second time.

ANYTHING but THAT

Flew alone for the first time.
☒ Check.

Pulled an all-nighter in an airport.
☒ Check.

Had a shock
like the one I had earlier today . . .

DEFINITELY NOT ON MY BUCKET LIST.
LIKE, NO WAY!

D234 **(EXPLANATION)**

VANCOUVER airport

My father had made me promise at least two hundred times to call him when I landed in Vancouver—probably to make sure I'd given up on my plans to run away. One long-distance phone call was all it took to reassure him I had just one thing on my mind:

ARRIVE in in ONE PIECE
JAPAN

"Dad, it's me. Sorry for waking you up. I just wanted to let you know, well, I'm alive."

"Hi, Franny! You're not waking me up, it's only 7 p.m. here. So, you had a good flight?"

"Yeah, it was fine, except for the old lady next to me who snored for five hours straight."

"See—you did that like a champ!"

"Sure, Olympic level."

"Are you still mad, sweetheart?"

"No. Maybe, I don't know . . . but I can't wait to see you."

"Me too."

"Can we at least order sushi?"

"All the sushi you can eat, I promise! I'll even bring some to the train station when I pick you up."

"What do you mean, the train station? You said you'd pick me up at the airport!"

That was when my dad put on his "I feel terribly guilty, but I'm still going to hit you with this bad news" voice:

"I know, sweetheart . . . But I need to stay here in Kyoto for work. But don't worry. I've taken care of everything, okay?"

Oh no.

When my dad says he's *taken care of everything*, that usually means:

"I'm sending a friend of mine to pick you up. Her name is Yoko. Cool?"

"Yo . . . what?"

"Yoko."

"Really? What kind of name is that? It sounds more like a vacuum cleaner brand."

"Franny, that's not very nice. Yoko's very excited to meet you. I've told her an awful lot about you."

". . ."

"All right, be careful, please. I'll see you soon."

"Uh-huh."

"Have a good flight, stink bug."

"Okay, bye, Dad."

Ten hours and 22 minutes + mega turbulence + frozen airplane food + all-you-can-eat peanut packs + a few rock-hard pillows later, I finally landed in Tokyo. It seriously felt like I'd just landed on another planet, but I'D PROMISED myself I wouldn't panic.

Franny, just focus on getting your suitcase
and finding your only hope of not becoming lost forever
in one of the biggest cities in the world,
namely:

After ten minutes of searching in vain, I sat down on my suitcase smack in the middle of the airport arrivals hall. As I watched the crowds milling around me, one thought kept running through my mind:

Dad.
I seriously can't believe it.
You forgot to tell me what this Yoko person even looks like.

Just as I was starting to seriously consider calling 911 to report my lunatic father to the Japanese authorities and request IMMEDIATE repatriation to Quebec . . . I heard a voice.

"Funny. Funny, please, come here!"

A woman, holding up a sign that said "FUNNY," was talking to me in some kind of weird Japanese-sounding English.

"Um, me?" I answered.
"Yes! You!" she carried on.
"Um, my name is Franny, by the way. FRAN-NY. Not Funny. There's nothing particularly funny about this situation."
"Yes, Funny."
"Whatever."

Twenty minutes later, the woman with the strange accent and I were seated side by side on a train, quieter than two Buddhist monks deep in meditation. Yes, you heard that right, Diary: I followed a total stranger onto a train—despite everything my father's always told me about "stranger danger."

To be completely honest, I figured the creep factor associated with this Japanese chick—dressed and made up like we were going to a wedding—was pretty low. As far as risks went, I decided the worst that could happen was I might be blinded by her fluorescent-orange-flowered dress (which looked an awful lot like wallpaper, come to think of it). Anyway, it's not like I had a choice. No plan B, no other options. Because everywhere I looked, everything was so . . . Japanese. The writing on the walls, the expressions on people's faces, even their clothes.

It's pretty simple here:

They speak Japanese,
they eat Japanese,
they walk Japanese.

AND I DON'T UNDERSTAND A THING.

Honestly,
for all I knew,
this train could have been
headed for the moon.

Anyway. I closed my eyes the minute I sat down on the high-speed train for Kyoto. I was on the world's fastest train, and I didn't even register how it felt to be moving at 250 miles per hour. That's how numb my brain was.

They don't call it the
"bullet train" for
nothing, Diary!

96

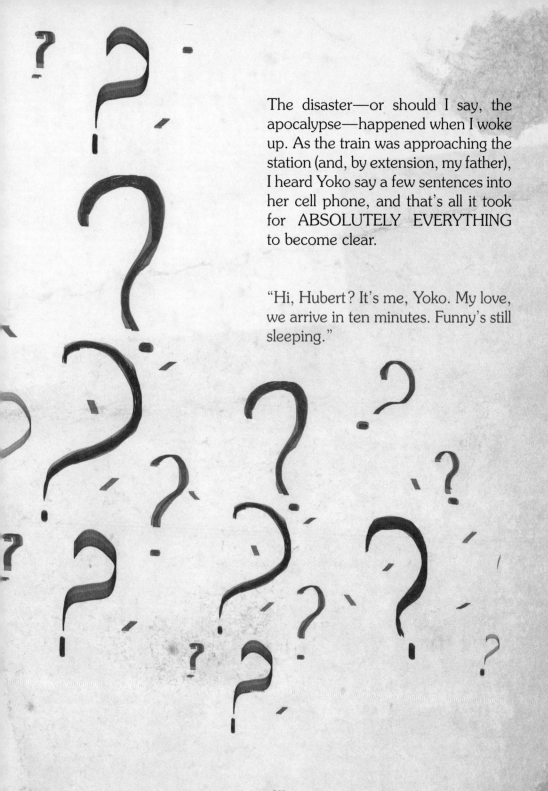

The disaster—or should I say, the apocalypse—happened when I woke up. As the train was approaching the station (and, by extension, my father), I heard Yoko say a few sentences into her cell phone, and that's all it took for ABSOLUTELY EVERYTHING to become clear.

"Hi, Hubert? It's me, Yoko. My love, we arrive in ten minutes. Funny's still sleeping."

Translation:
I have a Japanese stepmother and I'm stuck here for the rest of eternity? Um, no, I don't think so.

Tuesday, March 21, 7:15 p.m. (Japan time)
Arrival

Twelve minutes later, I was standing in front of my father and his toothy grin that was oozing pure happiness—happiness at finally having me back. Obviously, because of what I'd just found out, it left me completely cold. Even as he wrapped his arms around me, all I could think was: I'm going home to Sylvie and Leona as soon as possible. That's it: I'm leaving this country, whether my father likes it or not!

Yoko and I may not speak the same language, but she understood from the look on my face that things weren't exactly copacetic. She stepped far enough away so I could have a private conversation with the biggest liar in history—namely, my father.

"Franny! Finally! Oh, it's so weird to see you here, stink bug!"
"You can say that again."
"You must be tired, sweetheart."

" . . ."

"Okaaay! If you were this quiet with Yoko, it must have been quite the long train ride!"

"Dad, can I ask you a question?"

"Of course!"

"I bet you think this is really cute, eh?"

"What's that?"

"Oh, come on, Dad! You do know Yoko was the name of John Lennon's wife, right? And you're NO John Lennon. And she's NO Yoko Ono! In fact, you're nothing but a copycat who's 40 years behind the greatest songwriter in the history of pop!"

"Franny, you—"

"No, spare me your lame excuses. You KNEW there was no way I'd come here if you'd said you have a girlfriend. So, why don't you just admit it?"

"Franny, we'll talk about this at home."

"Home? What home? I don't see any home. All I see is a humongous country and a humongous lie that you had no right keeping from me! And now I'm stuck here."

"That's enough, Franny. We're leaving."

"Not like I have any other choice."

I tore my suitcase out of my father's hand and started walking three feet ahead of him, with Yoko-not-Ono trotting to keep up with us. From that point on, I didn't utter a single word, and I especially didn't shed a single tear.

Anyway, I don't have a single tear
left in me.
I've become an armored vehicle
of sadness.

On the way "home," I didn't even look up once at the passing scenery. I was dying to see everything, Diary—to at least get my bearings a little—but I didn't want to give *Mr. Man* the satisfaction. As it was, he spent the whole trip eyeballing me in the rearview mirror. I could tell he was hoping for a sign, a word, the tiniest scrap of hope that I'd eventually come around to his life in Japan.

SO...
I STARED
SUPER
INTENTLY
at my FEET.

32 minutes later, we were there.

The first thing I did, when I was finally alone in what my father had decided was "my room," was text Leona.

The Internet was down—yup, my dad's in for a MEGA phone bill with all these texts. But given the conversation I just had with Leo, I honestly have bigger things to worry about right now.

TEXT THREAD

MARCH 21, 4:20 a.m. Quebec time (oopsie)
// MARCH 21, 5:20 p.m. Japan time

Franny
Hey, Leo, it's me!!
I'm here.

Leona
OMG, that was fast!

Franny
Seriously? I left two days ago!!

Leona
Yeah, true. Everything okay?

Franny
NO.

Leona
You just got there, you can't be freaking out already.

Franny
It doesn't matter, I'm not staying.

Leona
What???

Franny

I'm coming back to St. Lorette!!! Big surprise, my dad lied to me AGAIN.
Now he'll have no choice but to listen to me.

Franny

We'll be together again soon, and I know this isn't something you usually say by text, but I had way too much time to think about it on the plane and . . . well, let's never let a guy come between us again. N-E-V-E-R.

Leona didn't reply. Which I found really weird. Abnormally weird, in fact. I mean, apart from the fact that I'd just texted her in the middle of the night, she should have been thrilled about our upcoming reunion.

Franny

Hey . . . why aren't you saying anything?

Leona

Huh?

Franny

Helllloooooooooooo???

Leona

It's the middle of the night, I'm just tired.
I'll write back later, okay?
Take care xx

Franny

Did you at least give Henry my letter?

Franny

Can you please just tell me if you gave him the letter?

BELIEVE IT
or not, DIARY,
LEONA
NEVER REPLIED
to my last text.

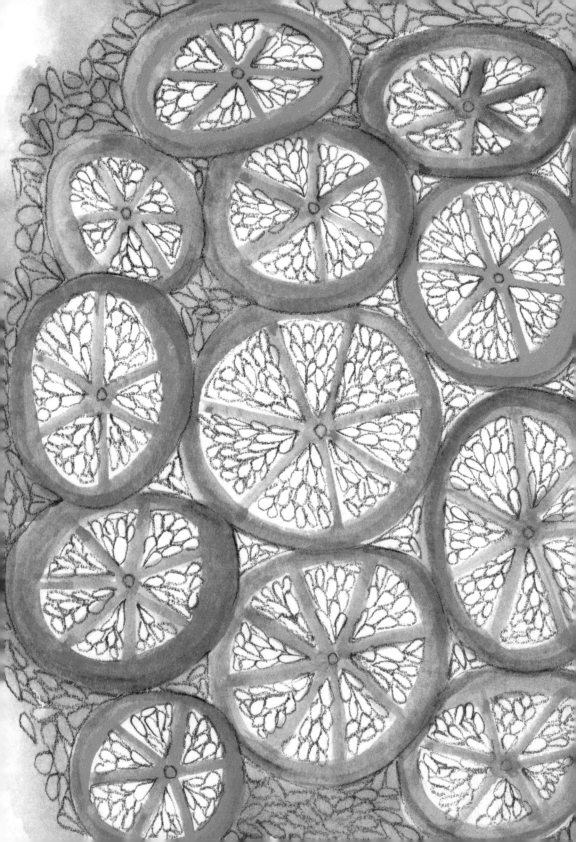

I'm going to keep texting her until she talks.

In the meantime . . .
I flew 6,312 miles only to land . . .
here.
I AM HERE
化粧品

A FEW FACTS ABOUT MY FATHER'S APARTMENT:

IT'S ① FREEZING
AND MINUSCULE

I swear, all the doors here are made of rice paper!

The only time I take off my winter coat is to take a bath.

+

The cracked beige paint
dates from 1940
(ugh, depressing).

② IT'S FILLED WITH NEW INVENTIONS

MADE BY MY FATHER, WHO'S CLEARLY OUTDONE HIMSELF WHEN IT COMES TO MAKING OUR LIFE MORE COMPLICATED.

Example: he's converted the toaster into some strange machine that can apparently make an entire breakfast on its own. Scrambled eggs, toast, coffee. Obviously, I have no clue how it works. I'm thinking I might starve to death here.

3

IT'S PERCHED
ON TOP OF
A SHOP OWNED BY
AN OLD LADY
WHO'S LIKE 150 YEARS OLD.

ALL SHE SELLS ARE LIPSTICKS
AND FACE POWDER.
PRETTY
SKETCHY.

Wednesday, March 22

NOW ←--- My father decides to act like a father.

"Yes, I knew it."

That's what my father had to say when he came to sit on the end of my bed at 7:00 this morning. At least he seemed ready to tell the truth. Unlike Leona, who, by the way, is still ignoring my texts.

"I knew you wouldn't want to come, Franny, if I'd told you . . . about Yoko."
"Well, that's not cool."
"I know."
" . . . "
"And I'm sorry. But I'm sure you'll like her, once you get to know her."
"That's going to be hard, Dad. She doesn't even speak French."
"She'll learn. And so will you."
"Learn what?"
"To speak Japanese one day . . . you never know."
"Um, no, I don't think so."

While the awkwardness passed, my father stared at the flowered wallpaper plastered all over my room. I couldn't help thinking, *We should tear it all down and make a huge dress for Yoko,* but I bit my tongue, because I was still too tired for that kind of banter. That said, I was awake enough to notice my father snooping through my suitcase on the floor next to my bed—subtly lifting the lid with his foot—probably to gauge how resigned I was to the thought of living here.

"Want help unpacking?"
"What for? I'm not staying."
"Franny."
"Sylvie will be happy to take me back, Dad."
"Forget about it. You're not living with her. We've always managed to get by, just the two of us! And I refuse to argue about this with you. You're my daughter, for God's sake!"
"Then start acting like a father!"

With that one sentence—actually, attack might be the better word for it—my father stood up like a shot, propelled by his pride straight

off the bed.

"Okay, then."
"What?"
"I'll show you how a father acts. And trust me, Franny, you won't soon forget it!"

My eyes flew open. Clearly, the situation had just gone sideways: when my dad jabs his index finger to within an inch of my nose, that's a sure sign he's working up to the comeback (or grounding) of the century.

CRAP. I just screwed up (ROYALLY).

"Tonight. Dinner at Dimitri's. He's my colleague, and he's invited us over whether you like it or not! So, you're going to get up, get dressed, put a smile on your face, and be ready at 5 p.m. sharp. Until then, I don't want to hear any more of your whining!"

"But, Dad, why do I have to go? I don't want to—"

"Franny Cloutier, CUT IT OUT! That's enough! It was a terrible idea to send you to St. Lorette. You've been impossible ever since!"

"I've always been impossible! So have you, by the way!"

"Okay, I've had just about enough of you. You can stay in your room for the rest of the day!"

"Hey! I'm not six years old!"

"Then stop acting like it!"

OMG, now my dad is stealing my comebacks
because he's too lame
to think up his own.

After dropping that bomb, he stalked off to the kitchen. I could tell he was worked up, because he started drying a pot that wasn't even wet. I'm guessing if I'd gone to apologize right then, he might have been willing to hear me out. But seriously, what was the point? For me to become his perfect little expatriate-friendless-loner daughter? Um, no thanks.

That's when I got what you might call
"the worst idea on the planet."

Only problem was,
I didn't realize it
at the time.

WORST IDEA ON THE PLANET
BY FRANNY CLOUTIER

Okay. I'll go to your colleague's lame dinner tonight.
But I promise you'll regret it, Dad.

*** PLAN ***
As long as he's forcing me to stay
here
I'll simply turn my father's
perfect life
into a living

NIGHTMARE.

 # Humiliation 101

Dad got the brilliant idea that walking to his stupid dinner would do me a world of good. So, I trekked halfway across the city next to my father, who was carrying a huge tray filled with about a hundred homemade cream puffs. He calls them his "whipped cream hot dogs."

"So, if you weren't my daughter, I'd swear you'd grown up in Kyoto."
"So, if you weren't my father, I'd swear you were a pastry chef."
"I say that because we've been walking for a half hour, and not once have you looked up or even asked a single question . . ."
"Yeah, so?"
"So, we're in one of the most beautiful cities in the world, Franny! You're not impressed, even a little?"

I have to admit my father was right. I refused to look at anything, kind of like a person with a peanut allergy won't go near a slice of peanut butter toast. I'm allergic to Kyoto, and paying the slightest bit of attention to the city, exotic or beautiful as it may be, would automatically be interpreted by my father as a sign that I'm giving in and make me a prisoner of this life (whew, that was a mouthful).

But I felt better knowing my plan was working so far. By that, I mean my father had no clue what I'd cooked up to ruin his evening—and with a little luck, his reputation. But he was seriously starting to get on my nerves with his observations.

117

"I think you went a little overboard, Franny."

"With what?"

"The makeup. I don't think I've ever seen you wear blue eye shadow, or lipstick."

"Maybe Japan inspires me."

"Hmmm. I hope it doesn't inspire you too much."

We (finally) got to Dad's colleague's house which, by the way, is at least a thousand times nicer than ours.

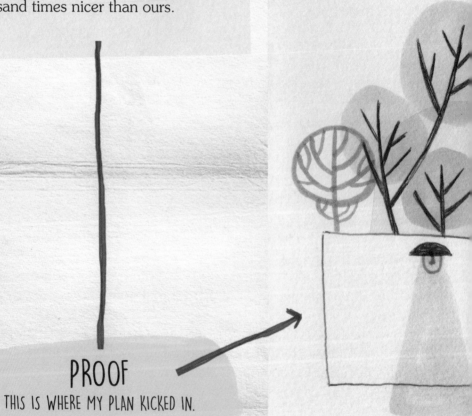

PROOF
THIS IS WHERE MY PLAN KICKED IN.

SAM'S HOUSE.

The second the door opened, I smacked the tray of cream puffs out of my father's hands, sending the desserts he'd spent hours making flying all over the entryway.

CARPET,
DOOR,
floor

AND EVEN:

our host's pants.

There was whipped cream and chocolate absolutely everywhere. Without even the hint of an apology, I barged into the house like a gawking tourist, tracking whipped cream everywhere. I even commented on the paintings hanging on the walls. My father, down on all fours, was sputtering out apologies.

"Dimitri, stop, you shouldn't have to clean that up. Franny, get back here! You're getting it everywhere!"

My father was glaring at me, but I didn't care.

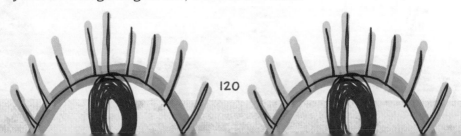

"Oops. Sorry . . . I wasn't looking where I was going. Oh, wow! That's a pretty impressive Van Gogh fake. You know he wasn't just a painter, right? He also kept a journal, like a diary, I mean. Oh? You didn't know?"

We'd been there a whole three minutes, but already my father's colleague—a snobby, old, half-bald intellectual wannabe in a suit and tie—had had enough of me. I had to wonder what offended him more: my massive arrogance or my Quebec accent, which he probably couldn't understand. I say that because Dimitri and his entire family are from Paris, by the way.

Anyway, everything went according to plan. Dimitri stood up and fixed me with a cold, mean stare, as much as to say, *Your father obviously didn't raise you right, I'll teach you some manners!* But it didn't slow me down even one beat—terrible, I know.

"So, Van Gogh here, he said painting was the thing he was least bad at. And that, basically, he was a terrible people person. Not a very sociable guy. Kinda like you, Dad, right? You might not know this, but my father likes to hide out with his inventions and would give ANYTHING to become famous . . . even his own daughter, I think, which should tell you something!"

My father was livid, but my mission was far, far from being completed. Under my winter coat, I was dressed as his WORST nightmare. So, here's what I was wearing under my bulky parka:

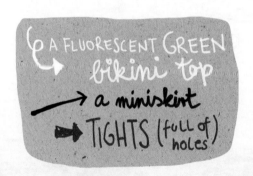

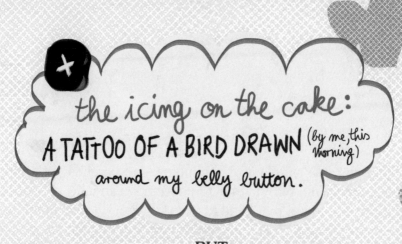

the icing on the cake:
A TATTOO OF A BIRD DRAWN (by me, this morning)
around my belly button.

BUT
IT BECAME VERY CLEAR THAT I—ALONG WITH MY BIKINI
AND MY RIDICULOUS TATTOO—HAD JUST
LOST THE WAR
AT THE PRECISE MOMENT THIS DAWNED ON ME
(as I happened to glance toward the kitchen):

Dimitri .... is my father's colleague.
Jeanne .... is my father's colleague's wife.
Sam .... is my father's colleague's SON.

That's right, Diary: Dimitri has a son my age. His name is Sam and—believe me—he's no normal guy. Nope. Not your average teenager.

Sam is the kind of guy who always looks like he's just stepped out of a magazine: mysterious eyes, perfectly red (but not too red) pursed lips, and a head topped with a phenomenal mop of light-brown wavy hair mussed to perfection. Like every part of his body was flawlessly designed, sculpted, and executed.

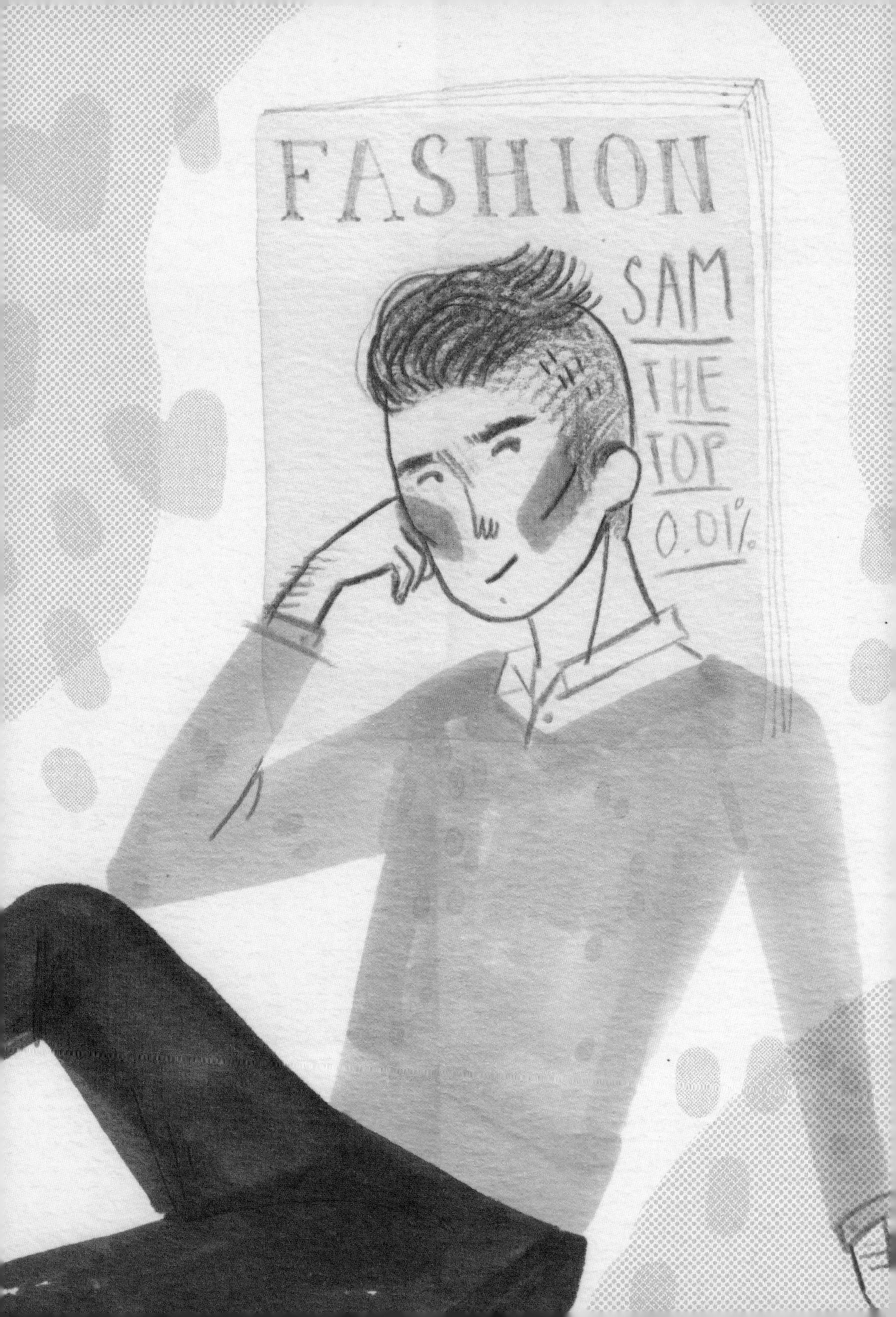
FASHION
SAM
THE
TOP
0.01%

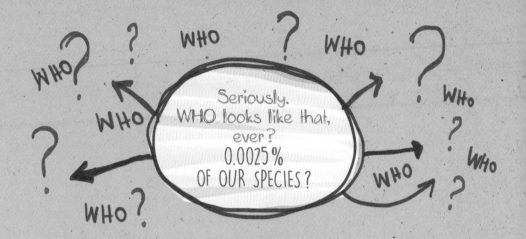

Seriously.
WHO looks like that,
ever?
0.0025%
OF OUR SPECIES?

WHO? WHO WHO WHO ? WHO WHO ? WHO ? WHO ? WHO ?

Mr. Perfect was leaned up against the hallway wall, earphones dangling around his neck (OMG, his neck), eyeballing me shamelessly. I'd just made a spectacle of myself, and he'd obviously enjoyed the show.

As he walked toward me, I thought, *Crap, Franny, find the closest window and RUN. For God's sake, a little pride, please!*

Too late.

Mr. 0.0025% a.k.a. Sam was right in front of me, his Parisian accent both dripping with sarcasm and oozing with kindness. Needless to say, I instantly lost it, turning into the biggest pile of mush. EVER

I swear.

Even my encounter with Henry
was a picnic
compared to what happened that night, Diary.

"Franny, is it? Something you should know about Japan is we always take our shoes off inside . . . like, everywhere. It avoids . . . tracking chocolate into people's houses."

My answer came out sounding like my brain had been soaking in whipped cream all day:

"Oh, really? It's just that I got here only yesterday, and, um, at home in Quebec, we, I mean . . ."

"Really like chocolate?"

"Take them off. Our shoes, I mean . . . I take my shoes off. Hey, Dad, leave that, I'll do it . . . I'll clean it up."

My father handed me the roll of paper towels without so much as looking at me.

"Darn right you will!"

Then he disappeared into the living room, along with everyone else. Everyone except for Mr. Perfect, who continued watching me clean up the huge mess I'd made in the hallway.

COMPLETE AND UTTER HUMILIATION

"And I guess . . . you don't take your coats off either, in Quebec?"

"Huh?"

"I mean I can take your coat for you. Here, give it to me, I'll hang it up."

"No! No, no, no, I'm cold. Freezing in fact, but thanks!"

"You're weird."

"I'm not weird. It's a thousand degrees below zero in your house."

"Fine, whatever."

Sam strolled off nonchalantly, hands in his pockets.

ARRGGGH

His too-chill,
relaxed-to-the-max, mister-nice-guy thing
was getting to me way too much.

I took a deep breath and thought:

Okay, Franny,
get a hold of yourself,
and come up with a plan,
because sooner or later, you're going to have to take off
this coat!

"Dinner's ready!"

Dimitri called us all
to the dining room table.

Yeah.
Table.

\ \\ / that's \ \ /
↑ SAYING ↑
⌐A LO⌐T⌐.⌐

Here in Japan (I guess I'll have to get used to saying that), on top of always using chopsticks, people eat sitting on the floor. I SWEAR, Diary! It's like the legs on every single table in the country were chopped off by someone with a terrible sense of humor.

I approached my father gingerly. But I knew NOTHING could make up for what I'd just put him through. Needless to say, my little act of rebellion had come to an end.

"We're going to talk about this, you and me. Don't ever think you can pull something like that again, Franny."
" . . . "

"I've never been so embarrassed in my life!"
" . . . "

"And in front of the only person who's ever believed in me, my entire career!"

"I'm . . . I'm so—"

"Franny, I highly suggest you keep your mouth shut."

"Okay. . ."

"Take a cushion and sit down right there."

"There?"

"There?" as in: Do I really have to sit next to Sam?

I was sweating bullets under my coat, and sitting right next to Sam clearly wasn't going to help matters! After twenty seconds, I was already red as a tomato. Jeanne and Dimitri set down a huge bowl of spinach fettucine right in front of us. I looked at Sam skeptically.

"Pasta?"

"You're hilarious. You say that like you think rice and sushi are the only things we eat in Japan."

". . ."

"I thought so too, at first."

I smiled. Sam was right: I admit, when I landed in Japan, I thought I'd seen the last of anything remotely resembling pizza or spaghetti. Even though my wardrobe disaster was far from over, and I had the sad-but-true feeling my father would never forgive me for what I'd just done, I felt better. Not so much because of the fettucine but because of him, because of Sam.

No sooner did I think that than another thought popped into my head. And this uninvited thought even had a name. It was .... Henry.

Crap. Every time I start to feel the least bit happy, his face appears in some part of my brain. This can't go on. I need to talk to Leona. I'll call her a thousand times in a row if that's what it takes to find out what's going on in St. Lorette.

Just then, my father's voice interrupted my thoughts, making me jump.

"Franny."

"What?"

"Take off your coat, we're about to eat."

"But, Dad, it's just . . . I don't think that's a very good idea."

"Franny, take off your coat this instant!"

"Fine . . . But don't say I didn't warn you."

TOTAL DISASTER
AHEAD

Just as I was about to slip off my coat under the quizzical gaze of Sam (and the still-furious glare of my father), I was saved by a knock at the front door. Dimitri stepped into the dining room, carrying a huge salad bowl.

"Sam, get the door, please."
"Never mind, Sam. Franny will get it! Isn't that right, Franny?"

I stood up, rolling my eyes at my dad's totally lame attempt to seem all parental in front of his colleague. I have to admit, when I opened the door, it took everything in me to control my reaction when I saw who was standing there, frozen solid in the doorway. Yup, none other than Ms. Wallpaper herself (apparently also known as *my father's girl-friend*). But since I'd already messed up enough for one night, I invited her in, with every last ounce of good manners left in me.

(Which wasn't much.)

"Well, come in, Yoko, I won't bite."
"Hello, Funny."
"It's Franny. My name is FRAN-ny."

What she said next caught me completely
off guard, because it came out . . .
in French. Or kind of.

"I late, *moi excuse.*"

"Huh? You speak French?"

"I try. A little . . ."

"Well, you're not too bad."

"Tinks."

"Hey, Yoko. Think you'd understand me if I, like, asked you a question?"

"Question, yes, yes."

"Okay. Well, I have a MEGA huge problem. Think you could help me?"

"You talk more slow, okay?"

And just like that, I had a brilliant idea. Well, okay, maybe not brilliant, but at least smart enough to keep me from . . . ruining the rest of my life.

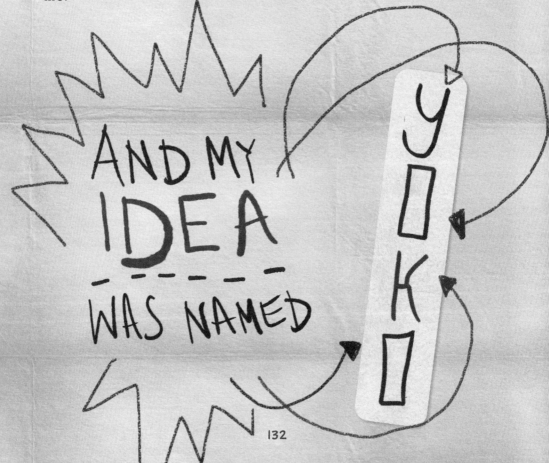

AND MY IDEA — — — WAS NAMED YOKO

Let's just say Yoko had no clue what was happening in that doorway, but when she realized all I had on was a bikini top, she agreed on the spot to lend me her gorgeous cashmere sweater. Yoko may not speak French, but I'm starting to think she's fluent in body language.

The rest of the night went pretty well, I think. I managed to act normally around Sam, who apparently no longer thinks I'm weird. I know that because, at the very end of the night, he invited me—drumroll, please—to a party on Saturday night!!!!

P.S. //
Um, just so we're perfectly clear: I'm still sad and upset. But the thought of having some fun with people my own age sounds a lot better than the alternative, which is spending my Saturday night cozied up with my father and his new girlfriend.

To be continued tomorrow . . .
(so I can fill you in on the party).

Franny
XOX

My first Japanese party! Yay!

Hey, Diary. So, I'm currently pretending to be asleep under my covers. That's because I KNOW after the stunt I pulled yesterday, my father isn't likely to be too forgiving this morning. He's so predictable, come to think of it. I can pretty much guarantee the second I poke my big toe out of bed, my father will call me to the kitchen table. Then, he'll hold out both hands and he'll want to talk.

And talk.
And talk and talk and talk.

See, my dad has this lame rule: whenever he wants to bawl me out, to make sure I really "get it," we're supposed to hold hands and look each other in the eye until HE decides the talk is over and I've learned my lesson and won't do it again. When he's finally done, he always says the same thing:

Then it's over.

— I can't wait until I'm 18 so I don't have to
deal with this anymore. —

Basically, I have zero interest in being bawled out, so I'm pretending to be asleep. My Japanese bed is very comfortable, by the way—see, I can admit when something's good!

Another good thing that bears repeating, if you ask me: last night, Mr. Perfect invited me to my first-ever party (anywhere—not just Japan)!!!

LET ME EXPLAIN.

The rest of last night's dinner went smoothly. Ms. Wallpaper, who wasn't really catching much of the conversation, spent the ENTIRE dinner teaching me how to eat fettucine with chopsticks, while Dimitri listened to my father talk about the state of his research on the whatchamacallit jellyfish.

Unlike me these past few months, Sam seemed super interested in my dad's research on how to stop the aging process, asking a ton of questions my father was only too happy to answer. Meanwhile, I felt just as lost as Yoko because I didn't understand a word they were saying.

It made me realize I have no clue what my father is actually doing here. And honestly, I was never that interested anyway. But seeing Sam so enthralled, I was forced to admit that even though my dad hasn't exactly been "father of the year" . . . I sure haven't been "daughter of the century" either.

But that's
NOT
what I wanted to tell you.

SO,
HERE GOES.

Toward the end of the meal, Sam's phone started blowing up. And since my social life here is about as dry as the Sahara Desert, I was dying to know what was so important that someone needed to talk to him so badly. So, I said quite possibly the lamest thing in history—but guess what? It worked!

"So . . . Seems like you're pretty hot stuff in Japan."
"Nah, it's only because I'm planning a back-to-school party."
"But it's March. Doesn't school start in September?"

Sam stopped texting long enough to look at me like:

Um, hello? What planet are you living on?

Then, my father, who'd caught part of our conversation, launched into this long-winded explanation—obviously in a desperate attempt to avoid another diplomatic incident on my part:

"You see, Franny just got here yesterday, and she and I—well, we've had a few little misunderstandings lately."
" . . . "
"Franny, I was going to tell you this tomorrow, but since we're on the subject . . . Oh, dear, how can I explain this . . . So, the school year in Japan actually starts the first week of April."

— ? —

I beg your pardon? I was starting school in a week?! I swear, if I'd been sitting on one, I'd have fallen off my chair right then and there. But instead of losing it, I mustered as much wisdom and tact—if not more—than the Dalai Lama faced with an intricate and TOTALLY unjust political situation. All I said was:

"Okay. Cool! Um, I gotta pee, Dad. Be right back."

I stood up very slowly and discreetly slipped outside.

I really, REALLY needed some air, Diary.

I sat down on the front step and watched the snowflakes land on my borrowed cashmere sweater, wondering how I would pull this off.

STARTING OVER

Starting over from scratch at a new school. I figured I'd have to go back to school sooner or later . . .

but in
a week?

Just as I was starting to work up the nerve to go back inside, the door behind me slid open. It was Sam. He sat down next to me, just like that, without saying a word. We watched the snow fall on Kyoto, and despite the circumstances, I was surprised to find the whole scene quite beautiful.

And it reminded me
of Henry.

But then Sam's Parisian accent reminded me
it was definitely not Henry
sitting next to me.

"Admit it—you never thought it would snow in Japan."
"True. You're right. How did you know?"
"Because I was surprised too, when we first got here. I've been here for two years now and . . . you'll see, you get used to it."
"It snows tons in Quebec. I'm pretty used to it."
"No, I'm talking about moving to another country. Living here, I mean."
"Oh. I really don't think I'll get used to it this time. This is the second time in a year my father has pulled this crap on me."

Sam looked shocked, and it felt good knowing someone was sort of in my corner.

"Are you serious?"
"Yeah, but it's my fault. I mean, when my dad told me I'd have to move here, I shut down. Refused to talk about it. So, it's not his fault I didn't know . . . about school."
"Wait. You moved to another country, and you didn't ask your father one single question?"
"Um . . . No."
"Not even one?"

I shook my head.

"Wow. You're weird."
"Not really! I'm very normal, you'll see. I mean, maybe you won't see because, well, maybe we'll never see each other again . . . or, we probably will, one day . . . I mean, our fathers do work together, but . . . oh my God, I talk too much . . ."
"Yeah, maybe."
"I know, I talk too much."
"No! I mean, you're right . . . We might see each other again, like, if you come to my party?"
"Me?"
"Of course you! Were you planning to stay shut up with your father for the next week in your tiny apartment? You'll go completely bonkers."
"It's just that . . . I don't speak a word of Japanese."
"You really don't know how things work here for people like us, eh?"
"People like us?"
"That's right, kids of foreigners."

I stared at him blankly, eyes as wide as saucers, like:

Um, nope.
I don't know anything about anything.

"Let's just say you won't be going to a normal school. Unless your dad is completely clueless, I'm sure he's registered you for the French Secondary School, so you'll fit right in."
"Hang on a second. You mean you're inviting me to a party with people our OWN age who speak FRENCH, and I'll be going to school with people who speak—"
"French, yes."
"Oh. Wow! Okay, that's the best news I've heard in forever!"
"I bet! So . . . you good for Saturday?"

Suddenly, I was at a loss for words, but not because I didn't want to go to the party. So, Sam and I just sat there, pretty much in total silence. But—unlike most other times—I didn't feel the least self-conscious. I smiled at Sam, which he apparently took as a yes, because he said:

"Want me to pick you up?"
"Sure, perfect."
"Should we go back inside? It's baltic out here."
"What?"
"It's freezing!"
"Oh, okay!"

I THOUGHT:
I may not speak Japanese,
but Sam clearly doesn't speak Québécois!

We went back inside. From the look on my father's face,
I could tell he was wondering what had me
grinning from ear to ear.

THE END.

(Oh nooooooo, I just thought of something: What if my dad won't let
me go to Sam's party because of what I did? Too bad, I'll run away
if I have to, but I'm GOING to that party, no matter what.)

P.S. //
Still no luck getting hold of Leona.
I just sent her four texts and . . . nada.
Really weird, you have to admit.

4 TEXTS

SENT 22 MINUTES AGO

Franny — 9:45 a.m.

> So, if I told you a really cute guy
> invited me to a party . . .
> would you write back??

Franny — 9:53 a.m.

> OMG, Leo.
> I don't know what time it is there, but I've been texting
> you for 4 days now and you haven't replied.

Franny — 9:56 a.m.

> I'm so stupid.
> Obviously, you've forgotten about me, just like
> Sophie did last year.
> Well, now I have the perfect reason to stop thinking
> about you — and St. Lorette — FOR GOOD.

Franny — 9:57 a.m.

> If you don't write back to me
> TODAY, Leona Gingras, don't even bother.
> I'm not that stupid, after all.

Later.
F. x

AHA!

AHA!

"Midnight, Dad"
"Ten o'clock"
"Eleven."
"Ten thirty."

"How do you expect me to make friends here if you force me to leave the party just when it's getting good?"

"Ten forty-five, AT the door."

"With a fifteen-minute leeway in case something . . . unexpected happens."

"Okay, but I'm picking you up right out front."

"No way!"

"Take it or leave it, Franny."

"Okay, but park down the block, and I'll come out when you text me. I don't want anyone to see you."

"Deal."

The fact that my father was letting me go to Sam's party on Saturday night—when I'd tried to ruin his career less than 24 hours ago—was a little suspicious. It was even too good to be true. And I couldn't help thinking (in fact, I was certain) that my father had an ulterior motive.

I was right. Five minutes after his "I'm a cool dad and I've forgotten to ground you into the next century even though you really deserve it" act, my father sat down next to me in the living room. On our heated sofa. That's right. Our house may be frigid, but our couch is toasty warm (thanks to this giant rectangular table-blanket thingy designed to keep your legs warm at all times). Hard to explain, but it's true.

Incidentally, I'm starting to understand why my father likes Japan so much:

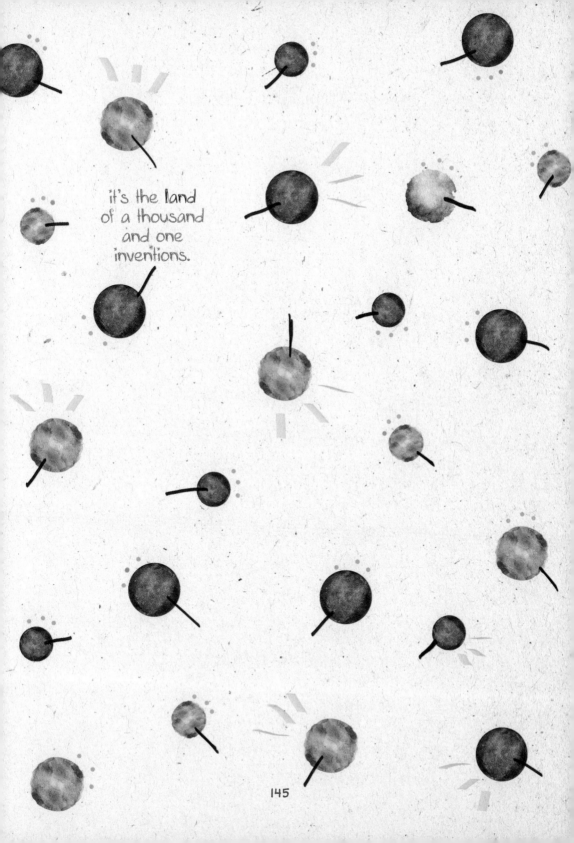

it's the land of a thousand and one inventions.

Like, just flushing our toilet is a major production. The first time I used it, I was scared one of the 250 buttons I pushed might accidentally launch me into space.

"What are you watching, sweetheart?"
"Japanese TV."
"Oh, it's a game show. You like game shows."
"Yeah, really helpful, the captions are all in Japanese."
"You can rent a movie if you want."
"What do YOU want, Dad?"
"I want to ask you something."
"Aha! I knew it! You didn't ground me yesterday because you want something from me. Ha! I'm so smart!"
"Sit down, Franny."

I sat down. I had no other choice: I value my freedom too much. And that's when my father told me I'd be meeting Yoko's mother on Sunday morning. Yup, you read that right, Yoko's mother.

"This is a country built on tradition. And according to tradition, I have to . . ."

"Yeah, I get it, meet Yoko's mother. But how exactly did I get roped into this tradition?"

"Simple. Because you're my daughter."

"Did I miss something? Did you guys get married without telling me? Because that wouldn't even surprise me. Wait, you didn't actually get married, I hope?!"

While I was busy freaking out, my father steered the conversation back on course.

"You know, Yoko asked me why you were wearing a bathing suit last night, under your coat. So, if I were you, Franny, I'd just say 'Yes, Dad, I'll put a smile on my face and come with you on Sunday even if I'm dead tired from my party.'"

I looked at him, as much as to say:

Seriously,
this crap of yours
is starting to sound an awful lot like blackmail.

But the thought of the party on Saturday night made me bite my tongue.

INVITATION TO MY
VERY FIRST
JAPANESE PARTY!!!

パーティーへようこそ

アーケード

(that wasn't so Japanese after all)

"Yesssss, Dad. I'll come with you on Sunday, and I'll put a smile on my face even if I'm tired from my party. But not if I'm dead tired. Cool? Can I watch my show now?"

"Yes, or . . . maybe we could talk about school for a sec?"

"No, I'm good, Sam filled me in."

"Oh, I see . . . Sam this, Sam that . . ."

"Um, no."

"Um, no."

"Stop copying me, Dad."

"Stop copying me, Dad."

Whenever my father acts goofy, it's his way of letting me know he's happy I'm there, under the same roof, in the same country as him. I just stared at my Japanese TV show.

I didn't want to rain on his parade.

F. xoxo

Sunday, March 26

Truth or dare?

(Saturday, 7:50 p.m.)

"It was really nice of you to pick me up, Sam. I mean, it would have been super awkward to show up alone."
"It's only normal."
"Um, no. Believe me. You should have seen the welcome I got in St. Lorette last year."
"Where?!"
"St. Lorette. Where I used to live, with my aunt Lorette."
"You mean your aunt's name is Lorette and the town you lived in was called . . ."

"St. Lorette, yup, you heard right. But even weirder, before my dad won the inventors' contest, I had no clue I had family there because he'd basically lied to me my ENTIRE childhood . . ."

As we walked through the snow-covered streets of Kyoto, I told Sam the whole story. About how nuts my life has been since my dad won that contest, about my mother, and even about all the stuff I found out about my family last year. I told him everything. Every last detail.

Well,
almost.

I left out the part about
Henry.

I couldn't bring myself to tell him about Henry. Couldn't even say his name, to be honest. And you know what, Diary? Don't be jealous, but it felt really good to say all those things out loud, for the first time ever! So, after twenty minutes of "Franny spills her guts," I suddenly came to a dead stop in the middle of the street, struck by a weird sense of déjà vu.

"Hey, Sam, didn't we come this way earlier?"
"Um, yeah. But it seemed like you still had a lot to say, so I . . ."
"You mean we've been walking around in circles? For real?"
"Um, yeah."
"I don't know if you realize it, Sam, but you're weird too."
"Yeah, probably a little . . . Hey, you're shivering. Here. Take my scarf."

As I stood there, letting Sam wrap his endlessly long plaid scarf around my neck, I couldn't help thinking Henry would die, absolutely DIE, of jealousy if he could see this now.

But you know what?
The truth is, I didn't care.

I would have even paid the paparazzi
two million dollars to film us
and post the video . . .

But let's get real. Fat chance the paparazzi would ever be interested in my life. So, I enjoyed Sam's scarf for what it was: a way to ward off death by hypothermia.

We started walking again—in the right direction this time and without me monopolizing the entire conversation. When I asked Sam to tell me about himself, I realized I wasn't the only one with a complicated family life.

"If you think your dad is a lot, you don't know mine."
"Oh, yeah? I thought he seemed cool . . ."
"Cool? My dad! Not really . . ."
"Why do you say that?"
"Let's just say he thinks I'm . . . a loser."

152

"You? A loser?"

"He's never come right out and said it, but I know he thinks it. I'm the biggest disappointment of his life—a son who's not like him."

"Well, you definitely have more hair than he does . . ."

Sam laughed, but I could tell his heart wasn't in it. So, instead of trying to be funny, I aimed for philosophical.

"I think it's good to be different from our parents. I feel like it's proof the human race is evolving."

OMG, Franny Cloutier,
what's with the stupid comments tonight?

"Yeah, I guess, but I don't really feel like talking about him . . ."

"That's fine, but it really doesn't bother me, Sam. You can say whatever you want. I'll listen."

Just then, without another word, Sam stopped dead. We watched silently as three women, draped in billowy, floral silk kimonos (kind of like Yoko's dresses, but more regal), with skin as white as porcelain, glided past us not three feet away.

"Those are geishas, Franny."

"Wow. Real ones?"

"Yup. Your father didn't tell you? They almost all live in our part of town, in Gion."

"No, I had no idea! I didn't even know our part of town was called Gion."

"You crack me up."

" . . . "

I'd heard about geishas before, but even so, I decided to ask Sam for HIS version of the facts.

GEISHAS

Basically, Sam explained that geishas are women
who are taught from a very young age how to master
different art forms (like dancing, singing, and music),
on top of how to act in a very specific
and, let's say, traditional way (AT ALL TIMES).

They often spend many years living with other
geishas-in-training.

Oh, yeah, and you can easily spot them on the street because of their porcelain skin, their painted red lips, and their silk kimonos, which (according to Sam) cost more than a wedding dress.

Sam told me there are only about 200 geishas* left in the
world and, apparently, they almost all live
in Kyoto.

*In the 19th century,
there were 17,000 of them!

And that's your history lesson for today. :)

Because, anyway,
as suddenly as
they appeared,

the three geishas
faded into

the blackness of an alleyway.

156

— HERE AND NOW —

I could have listened to Sam talk about geishas all night. But just as I was thinking we had a party to get to, after all our twists and turns, we were suddenly there.

"Here we are."

Franny, I told myself, THIS is your one and only chance at a social life. So, even though diplomatic incidents have kind of become your thing, don't even THINK about doing anything tonight that might make you the latest "reject of Kyoto."

— PLEASE —

ANYWAY. We stepped inside a huge eight-story building blazing with lights—a stark contrast to the deserted streets we'd just walked through.

The second we walked in, I felt like we'd been teleported to Las Vegas! I didn't know where to look—flashing lights, plushie machines, video games. It was completely nuts!!! And I was clearly the ONLY person who had no clue what was going on.

Sam explained that we were at an arcade and that his party was on the sixth floor, in a small, dark private room with glass and mirrors everywhere.

Be brave, Franny. Anyway; there's no turning back now.

We went straight up to the sixth floor, where Sam handed me a bracelet—our pass for the night. I'd never seen anything like it before. Obviously, the Japanese are light years ahead of St. Lorette when it comes to party planning. (Awesome!)

(1-0 JAPAN)

"This bracelet will let you play all the arcade games you want. I can show you how they work. Just be careful not to get lost if you go to another floor, because just about everything's in Japanese here!"

Ugh. As I glanced over the railing, the full meaning of the expression "culture shock" hit me like a ton of bricks. It was hard to believe a place like this even existed. Spread out over eight floors—EIGHT FLOORS!!!—and right before my very eyes, hundreds of kids were riveted to their arcade games, playing like their lives depended on it. Even though I'm not a big video game fan (like, not at all), it was by far the most exotic thing I'd ever seen in my life.

Earth to Franny.
Earth to Franny.

Apparently, Sam was talking to me,
but I hadn't heard a word he'd said!

"Ready?"
"Um, yeah, sure! Hey, Sam . . ."
"What?"
"Why exactly are you being so nice to me?"
"What do you mean?"
"Um, never mind. . ."

We'd just stepped into the private room, so I decided my compliment
could wait until later. "Instant Crush" by Daft Punk was blaring, and I
couldn't see more than three feet in front of me for all the gold balloons,
multicolored streamers, and other decorations hanging from the
ceiling. It was by far the biggest party I'd EVER been to! (Okay, the
only party . . .)

THE BIGGEST PARTY OF MY ENTIRE LIFE!

(DAFT PUNK rocked!)

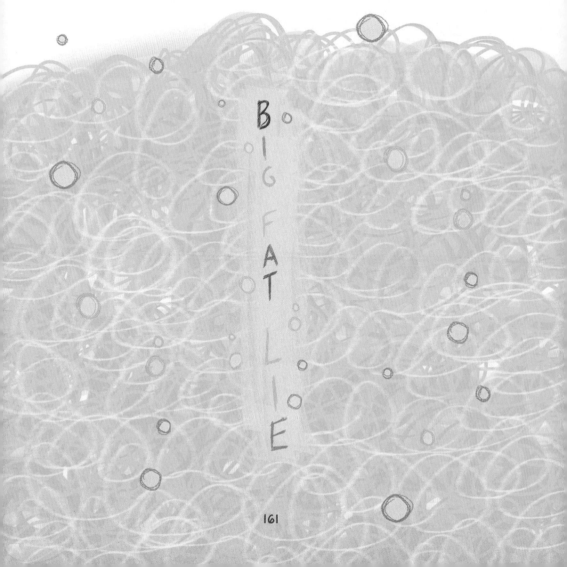

"Want me to put your beer with mine?"

Beer? Crap.
I hadn't even thought about that.
Well done, Franny, well done.

"Shoot! My beer! I forgot it at my dad's."

BIG FAT LIE

"No worries, I brought extra. You can help yourself to mine. I'll go find a bottle opener. You okay by yourself for a few minutes? I'll introduce you to my friends when I get back!"
"Of course, I'll be fine. Go!"
"Okay!"

The truth is, I was ~~freaking out~~ at the thought of being abandoned at a Japanese/not-so-Japanese party.

But so far,
everything was going surprisingly well.

Too well,
in fact.

It didn't take long for things to get complicated. For me to become acquainted with the source of all my future problems—at school, in this city, in my life—namely:

"Hey!"
"*Bonsoir.*"
With a Parisian accent, I must add. Barf.
". . ."

All right, I thought. Not the friendliest girl. I'd only been trying to break the ice and let her know quickly where I stand, like, *You'll see, I'm super nice, and you and your sophisticated French accent don't scare me, and let's be friends . . . okay?"*

F-A-I-L.

Just from the way she was staring at me,
I knew this girl had already labeled me an "in-betweener."

Incidentally, I thought the rule was that
you have to say at least one
complete sentence
before being labeled?
Apparently not.

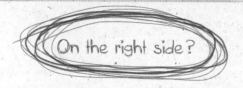

An in-betweener

Essentially, a student in this category
is neither a cool kid nor a reject.
They are, as the name implies,
somewhere in between.

On the right side?

The popular kids don't bother with them, and they still have friends.
The downside? They don't really exist in the eyes of the cool kids,
and—barring some bizarre social shift—
an in-betweener will never date a cool kid
and will (almost) never go to their parties.

P. S.
When I think about it, all these stupid rules
sound an awful lot like
the laws of the jungle.
The lions might think they're the most powerful,
but everyone knows the elephants are
the smartest,
AND SO
it's the elephants that are really
at the top of the food chain.

I'LL BE AN ELEPHANT.

That's right. I couldn't care less about this Capucine chick, not to mention all the other girls of her species. I am and always will be an "in-betweener."

But I couldn't help it, the longer I looked at her, the more tempted I was to say something like:

"Oh, wow,
I bet you're just as boring as your pasty lipstick."

But don't worry, Diary, I didn't say anything (bad, that is).

"I'm Franny. And you're . . . ?"
"Isn't that Sam's scarf around your neck?"
"My neck? Um, I . . ."
"Who are you, exactly?"

OKAY, LITTLE MS. SNOOTY. YOU OBVIOUSLY DON'T KNOW WHO YOU'RE MESSING WITH. IF IT'S WAR YOU WANT, IT'S WAR YOU'LL GET!

"I just told you, my name is Franny. And if you must know, I'm wearing his scarf because—"

I didn't have time to finish my sentence, because just then Sam showed up.

"She's wearing my scarf because it's cold out, and when it's cold out, people wear scarves to keep warm, Capucine. Cool? That all right with you?"
"I guess so."

PFFT. CAPUCINE.. SOUNDS LIKE CAPPUCCINO, IF YOU ASK ME.

~~CAPPUCCINO?~~

CAPUCINE

Capucine has long, thick hair, and she's a redhead. And she clearly thinks the lush, auburn tresses that follow her around everywhere she goes make her pretty special.

Capucine is also tall. I mean, really, really tall. Like, model tall. And another tiny detail I noticed right away: next to hers . . .

. . . my boobs look like they forgot to go through puberty.

Let's just say this Capucine person has the confidence of one of those people who's blessed with better-than-average looks. And (no doubt about it) I picked the wrong guy to borrow a scarf from tonight.

Sam handed me a beer.

"Come, I want to introduce you to someone."
"Okay."

I swear, if Sam hadn't grabbed my hand and led me away, Cappuccino would have strangled me right then and there with his scarf. On the bright side, even though there must have been at least fifty of us crammed into that pitch-black room, Sam and I managed to steal away together, alone.

(But not for long.)

My dad's calling me.
He says he wants to tell me something important about . . .
Hang on, I can't quite hear him.

Ah.
He says it's about breakfast at Yoko's mother's house.
Crap, I'd forgotten about that.
Yoko's mother.
This morning.
Ugh.

All right, I'll be right back . . .
I'm just going to see what he wants.

(. . .)
Stay tuned for the rest of the party recap.
Back in 5 minutes!

Okay! I'm back. So, as I was saying, Sam and I weren't alone for very long. Because, apparently, he was really obsessed with introducing me to one of his friends.

"Leif! Get down here! Crap, he can't hear us."
"Probably because he's standing on a table doing karaoke!"

Despite the place being hotter than a sauna, a guy wearing a powder blue sweater (that looked like it had been knitted by his grandma) was dancing while belting out Daft Punk in front of a karaoke screen. He stepped down, dripping with sweat, and greeted me with just the hint of a foreign accent, like we were old friends.

Leif: *Mon Dieu*, it's just impossible to sing Daft Punk. *Bonjour!* Franny, is it?
Me: You know . . . my name?
Leif: I also know you fling chocolate all over people's houses the first time you visit them.
Sam: Ah, Leif, that was uncalled for, man.
Leif: Not funny. *D'accord*, got it.
Me: No, that's okay, you're not wrong. I'm the girl who got chocolate all over Sam's house. And your name is Leif, like, um, a leaf?
Leif: Yeah, something like that.
Sam: Leif is from Iceland. That's why he always wears wool sweaters.
Leif: Hey! Leave my *très beau* sweater out of this. My grandmother made it.
Me: Aha! I knew it! I figured that as soon as I saw you.
Leif: *Vraiment?* You don't like it?
Me: No, I love it! And I love grandmothers too. Wait a minute, what am I saying? I've never had a grandmother. But, really, how could anyone hate grandmothers, I mean . . . I love pretty much, um, all grandmothers.

When I get verbal diarrhea like that, it's usually because I'm happy. Weird, I know. But just as I was starting to think, *Hey, I could get used to these Japanese parties,* Leif went ahead and proved me

Leif: Okay, Franny, *vas-y*, it's your turn to sing.
Me: Um . . . what? Nooooo, no way. Trust me, you don't want to see that, I—
Leif: You don't know Daft Punk? Really, all you need to say is "Lose yourself to dance"!

I looked at Sam, my last hope of getting out of this situation.

"Sam, please tell me I have a choice."
"Mmm . . . I don't think so!"

So, I took a deep breath, pulled off my sweater—at least I'd look somewhat cute in my tank top—and took the biggest swig of beer in history. Three seconds later, I was standing on a table, screaming:

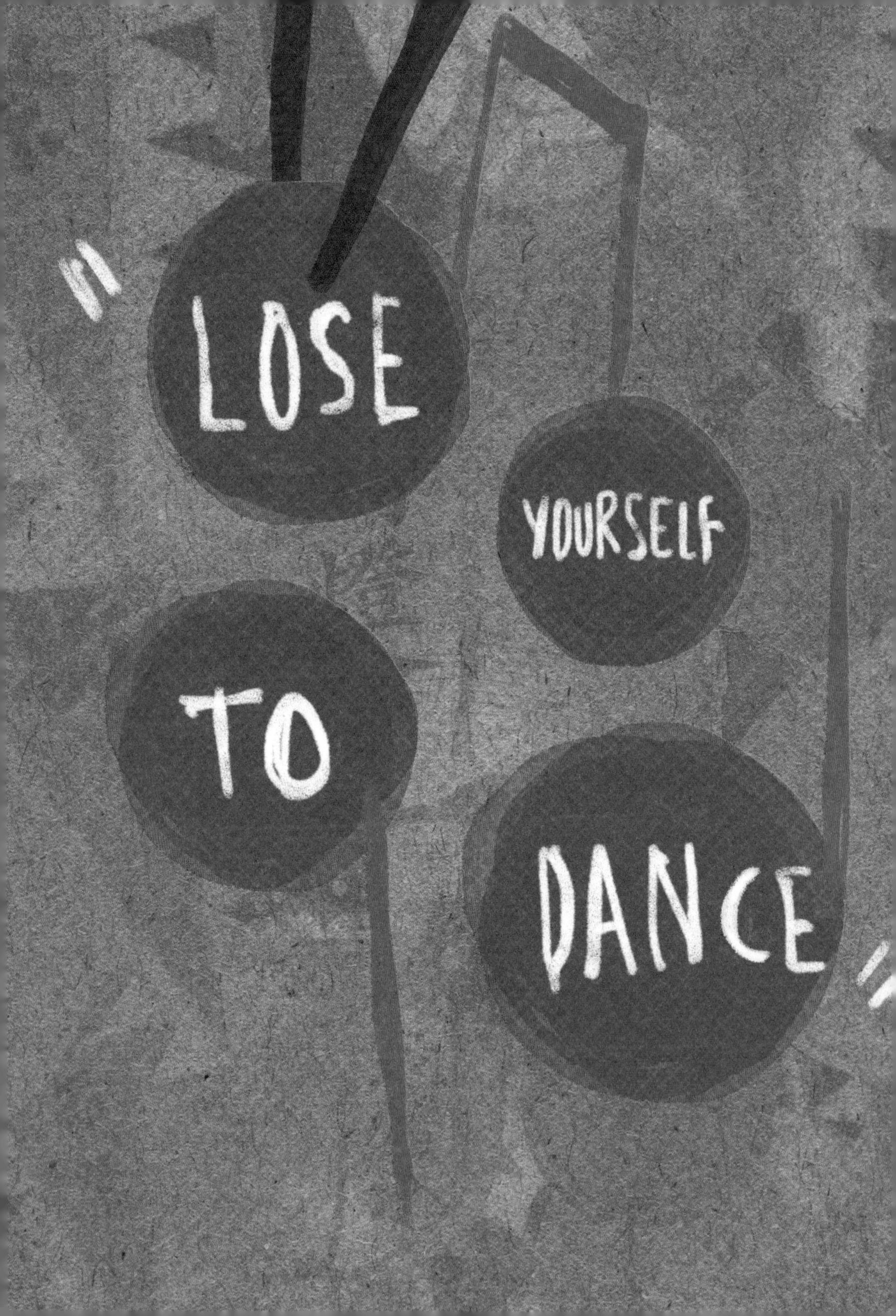
"LOSE
YOURSELF
TO
DANCE"

My father can NEVER find my diary, because he'd kill me if he ever read this. Um, literally. But I NEED to write it all down, otherwise it's not a REAL diary. Right. So, later that night, Sam started handing out tiny glasses filled with a syrupy liquid so strong it made my eyes water. All I can say is, from that moment on, every remaining ounce of embarrassment I had was gone:

 — LONG, LONG GONE. —

Leif and Sam and a bunch of other people—whose names I've already forgotten—were all wearing these funny Hawaiian garlands around their necks and dancing up a storm. Seriously, it was a little insane. But then (just as I was starting to think I might actually have a shot at a singing career, that's how natural I felt up on that table), I felt something vibrate in my back pocket.

My phone.

9:45 p.m.

It couldn't be my father; it was still way too early. My heart nearly burst out of my chest when I realized it was Leona texting me.

Leona—8:41 a.m., St. Lorette time

> I want to talk to you, I swear, but just not yet. Give me 24 hours, okay?

Leona—8:44 a.m.

> Franny? Why aren't you answering? Where are you?

I got down off the table and signaled to Sam that I needed to use the bathroom. I could tell he knew something had just happened; it was hard to miss from the way my expression had suddenly gone from euphoric to sad. In the bathroom, I sent a massively long text back to Leona.

Franny — 9:47 p.m., Kyoto time

> OMG, you have some nerve. Seriously, you're freaking out because YOU had to wait 2 minutes for ME to reply? I've been waiting 4 days for you to write back! I can only send you ONE text, because it costs a fortune, so pay attention. I'm at a party, I can't talk to you, and I'm not at all myself. Relax, I'm not on anything, I just drank this weird shot. Anyway, you'd better call me on Sunday, and you'd better have a really good explanation. Bye.

"Hey, are you writing a thesis over there, or what?"

Cappuccino was standing in front of the mirror, reapplying her deathly pale lipstick, watching me out of the corner of her eye.

"Yes, actually, a thesis all about little snobs like you."
"Oh, a rebel."
"What? Ha ha! I don't think anyone's said 'rebel' in the past fifty years."
"And I bet you think your accent is super classy too."
"What I think is that you should leave me alone. If you're worried I'll steal Sam away from you, you can relax, that'll never happen."
"I never said that."
"Capucine, is that it? Well, I'm seeing someone back home in Quebec. That's right. I have a boyfriend, and his name is Henry. Okay? Got it? So, you can have your Sam."

Yup.
I actually said that.

174

I said it because I just wanted her to leave me alone. I said it because I didn't have the energy to start over at a new school and deal with the mood swings of a princess like Cappuccino. And it worked. She shut up and disappeared back to the party. And I did the same. I was determined not to let her or Leona ruin my first party.

When I got back to the spot where I'd left Sam and Leif, the karaoke stage had turned into a sort of tearoom—but not quite. Leif turned down the volume, and a dozen or so people sat down on the floor in a big circle.

I had no idea what to do with myself, so—bad idea—I sat down with them. Leif's cheerful mood was even scarier than the karaoke machine.

Leif: *Bon*. Who wants to start?
Blonde girl sitting next to me: Sam, the party was your idea, you should go first.
Sam: No way, I hate these kinds of things.

THESE KINDS OF THINGS? Just as I was starting to seriously wonder where this party was going, everyone started chanting:

Sam heaved a big sigh and sat down on the floor. Big surprise, Cappuccino sat down right in front of him. Then she handed him a bottle.

Cappuccino: Truth or dare?

> Oh no.
> Danger ahead, Franny.
>
> That's what I thought to myself,
> but for reasons I find hard to explain, I just ...
> sat there.

Sam: Okay, whatever, truth.
Cappuccino: Hmm . . . interesting.

Cappuccino was holding a baseball cap, which I only realized later contained dozens of small slips of paper with questions written on them. Her face was beaming with satisfaction.

Cappuccino: So, is there anyone in this room you're attracted to?
Sam: . . .

> Sam didn't want to
> answer the question.

We all knew it, because at that exact moment, he turned to Leif and me (but more me, I think, even though Leif was sitting right next to me). And then, **I SWEAR TO YOU**, he just stared at me for a super long time. And by that, I mean at least five or even seven whole seconds. And believe me, Diary, it felt like an eternity in that moment. And the only semi-intelligent thing I could think to do was . . . stare at my feet.

Cappuccino: Come on, Sam. Are you acting shy in front of the new girl? You have to answer, that's how the game works.

Sam grabbed the bottle
and set it down
in the middle of the circle.

Too late.

Cappuccino had seen Sam staring at me—I mean, even a flea brain would have realized what was going on.

And I could tell in a flash how badly it had hurt her. And I don't just mean her ego was bruised. Her heart too. And I felt bad. Really bad. Like when someone has gone to the trouble of buying you a really thoughtful Christmas present, but then you ruin the surprise by guessing what's in the box. Okay, terrible analogy, I know, but it's all I got right now.

Moving right along.

Sam spun the bottle. I knew how this game worked. I knew that when the bottle stopped, he'd have to kiss the person in front of him. And just as I was thinking *What if it stops on me?* the bottle came to rest on none other than:

CAPUCINE.

Sam leaned toward her without even standing up. Then he kissed her. And you know what, Diary? The second their lips met, it all became crystal clear:

It was plain to see they'd done
this . . .
a million times before.

Their kiss was absolutely
nothing
like your typical first kiss.

I mean, the whole thing was way too neat, too practiced. Like they were two veteran ballet dancers, mere months away from retirement, capable of dancing a duet with their eyes closed.

Cappuccino savored the moment like a kid who's just been told she's holding

THE LAST ICE CREAM CONE ON THE PLANET.

GAG.

If I'm being honest, when their lips finally parted, I realized I was jealous. And Leif looked just as annoyed as I was.

Leif: She'll never get over him.
Me: I can see that.
Leif: *Ne t'inquiète pas* . . . she had her chance.

NE T'INQUIÈTE PAS.

It means "don't worry." I can tell you one thing, Diary: I didn't have to worry for very long, or kiss anyone, for that matter. Because, at that exact moment, my father texted me. And this time, the party really was good and over for me.

Dad   10:35 p.m.
> The ball's over, Cinderella ;)
> I'm leaving now.

Franny 10:37 p.m.
> Cool. Cinderella's ready to go home.

Dad   10:37 p.m.
> Everything okay?

Franny 10:37 p.m.

Yeah, yeah.
Just come get me, okay?

Cinderella

I left the party thinking about her.

When you think about it, she left all alone too, the night of the ball. Even after the prince had insisted on dancing with her, planting all kinds of ridiculous fantasies in her head. Whatever. Everyone knows the prince wouldn't have given her a second glance if he'd known what she really was.

A perfectly
ordinary
girl.

Slave to her family's wishes.

Come to think of it, Cinderella's claim to fame may have been forgetting her glass slipper on the front steps of a castle, but I made my mark on Kyoto while trying to find my coat in an arcade cloakroom. That's right. The tiniest, most chaotic cloakroom in history!

LET ME EXPLAIN. It was pitch dark, and even though hiding out in closets is normally my thing, this one really wasn't doing it for me. I just wanted to get away from that stupid party and go to bed. That's when I heard his voice. Sam's voice.

"You're leaving already?"
"Yeah. It's the time change. I'm still on Montreal—"

And that's when it happened. I didn't even have time to finish my sentence before I found myself horizontal on a pile of winter coats, thinking maybe this party wasn't so stupid after all.

Wrapped in Sam's arms, I forgot all about Cappuccino and Cinderella and even my father, who sat freaking out in his car for thirteen whole minutes, waiting for me to come out (don't worry, there was no danger of him turning into a pumpkin). Basically, what I'm trying to say is . . .

we didn't need a bottle,
or even a single one of the hundreds of lights
twinkling on the eight floors above us . . .

we just kissed.

Maybe not like two ballet dancers
in the twilight of their careers,
but still really well.

SAM and ME

Him: So, I guess I'll see you at school next week?
Me: Yeah, if we ever get out from under this huge pile of coats. *Lame joke, but whatever!*
Him: Yeah . . . and if your dad didn't register you for the Japanese school.
Me: Ugh!! Don't say that, it would be just like him to mess up like that!
Him: Nah, don't worry. All right . . . see you!
Me: Yup . . . bye.

I KNOW EVERYTHING'S MOVING AT 200 MPH here.

Do you think what's happening to me is normal, Diary?

I mean, less than two weeks ago, I couldn't even drag myself out of bed because I literally couldn't stop thinking about Henry. Then, last night, I let Sam kiss me like my heart was some kind of indestructible race car. Diary, please tell me I'm not suffering from some kind of love amnesia?

— That is a thing, right? I'm sure I didn't just make it up. —

CAN FALLING IN LOVE AGAIN MEND A BROKEN HEART?

Kind of like when you're making spaghetti sauce . . . And you add too much salt, so then you dilute it with tomato juice.

Can you dilute . . . love?

I'm being silly, I know.
Franny xo

Perfect recipe
By: FRANNY CLOUTIER

FOR GETTING OVER YOUR FIRST HEARTBREAK

INGREDIENTS:

↳ PERSEVERANCE
↳ TIME
↳ DISTRACTION!!!

 INSTRUCTIONS:

A) MOVE (IDEALLY TO THE OTHER SIDE OF THE WORLD).

2) MEET SOMEONE INTERESTING AND PERFECT IN EVERY WAY.

3) CUT ALL TIES WITH YOUR FIRST LOVE
(EVEN THE MENTAL ONES).

4) THROW AWAY ALL SOUVENIRS (WARNING: YOU'LL LOSE
A SMALL PART OF YOURSELF IN THE PROCESS).

* NOTE: IF YOUR FIRST LOVE WAS ALSO YOUR BEST
FRIEND, YOU'RE REALLY UP THE CREEK.

I really don't want to talk about what just happened. Let's just say, Leona may be a big fat liar, but what she said about letters is true:

Things sound even sadder when you write them down on paper.

I'm sorry
I can't write now,
Diary!
In the meantime,
you can read the rough copy
of the letter Leona
was supposed to give to Henry!

If I'd known then what I know now, I would have NEVER kissed Sam last night. Now Henry and I really are over, and it's all her fault. I'm NEVER going back to St. Lorette.

Letter
to Henry

Monday, March 20

Dear Henry,

I'm leaving for Japan in two hours. I know you don't want to hear my voice, but I'm hoping you won't mind reading my words.

Please, read this letter right to the end.
I swear, I won't ever ask you for another favor.
I'm starting to think your mother was right when she compared us to Romeo and Juliet. Our love story was

short,
star-crossed,
but beautiful.

Don't you think? Probably not anymore. Anyway. I'm writing you this letter because I suspect your mother might have been the one who sent me all those texts, on Valentine's Day. I'll say it again: I swear, I NEVER wanted you out of my life. Not even for a fraction of a second. Yes, it's true, everything happened really fast between us after Tommy's accident, but . . . you know what? I was never scared, because . . . well, because it was with . . . you. And because it felt right, and I felt like myself with you. Completely. Ugh, I miss you so, so, so much.

Please don't stop reading yet. I promise I'm almost done. When your mother kicked me out, I forgot to sign out of my accounts on the house computer (Facebook, Skype, Hotmail, AND my phone). And I feel terrible accusing her (oh, who am I kidding? I don't feel bad at all), but I'm sure, 110% certain even, that SHE'S the one who sent all those messages, to try to drive us apart.

I just wanted you to know that. If there's even a one-in-a thousand chance you might believe me . . . then it was worth it. I'll miss you in Japan.

I miss you already.
Everywhere, all the time.

Franny xx

Goodbye, Leona.

It's taken me four days to regain the power of speech,
but my brain is operating at a relatively
normal speed at the moment,
and I'm ready to try to tell you everything that's happened,
Diary.

Where should I start?
The good news
or the bad?

GOOD

BAD

I FINALLY KNOW
WHO SENT
HENRY THOSE
TEXT MESSAGES.

KEEP READING, YOU'LL UNDERSTAND.

TEXT THREAD

MARCH 25, 9:35 p.m. Quebec time
MARCH 26, 10:35 a.m. Japan time

Leona
Hello. If you're there, answer me. I'm ready to talk now.

Franny
Finally! What's your problem, ignoring me like that?!!

Leona
I didn't know how to tell you what I have to say.

Franny
Why? What's going on?

Leona
I did something.

Leona typing, erasing, typing, erasing, while I freaked out.

Leona
I can't say it. I just can't.

I stood up in a rage. I opened my laptop, and three and half seconds later, Leona's Skype started ringing on the other side of the world. The second she answered, I knew it was something serious. Her face was beet red (scalded by her tears?).

— I could smell the guilt from more than 6,000 miles away —

"Let me guess. You didn't give Henry the letter."
"No."
"Why not?"
"Because."
"Spit it out, Leona. No matter what happened, I'll find a way to fix it. Okay? I'm kind of a pro at fixing things now."
"You promise?"
"Promise what?"
"You won't get mad if I tell you the truth. And you'll let me finish before you start screaming at me?"

When someone says something like that
before making a confession,
it's never a good sign.

I said yes, but without really considering the implications of my answer.

I watched as Leona sat down on the end of her bed, her laptop perched on her knees. I waited for her to start talking. Waited with a horrible feeling that her endless deep breath would be followed by some terrible pronouncement. Her voice was shaking like a leaf.

"It wasn't Lorette who texted Henry to tell him to stop calling you."

"Excuse me? You read the letter I wrote to Henry?!"

"You said you'd let me finish."

". . ."

"It was me."

"What?"

"It was me who took your phone, on Valentine's Day."

". . ."

"And then I deleted the conversation . . . afterward."

". . ."

This was followed by a long, loooooooooooooooooooong silence.

"That's not all."

". . ."

"I also told Lorette that you and Henry kissed, on the night of Tommy's accident. Andre never said a word."

"Are you completely insane?"

That's all I could manage to say. I was too dumbstruck by the tsunami of confessions that had just slammed into me—and what remained of our friendship—to say anything else. Every line on my face was screaming I HATE YOU.

"Why? Why would you do that? Tell me!"

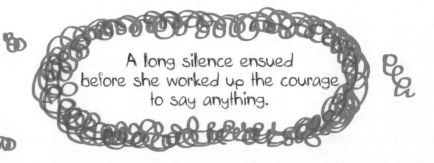

A long silence ensued before she worked up the courage to say anything.

But each time it seemed like an explanation was about to surface, it's like it got marooned somewhere between her, me, and the Pacific Ocean.

"I just wanted to have what you had."

"And what was that?"

"Someone. Someone who thinks I'm pretty. And special. And . . . well, it'll never happen, because no one ever looks at me that way."

"It'll never happen because you're stupid! Do you realize what you've done?!"

"What about you? You and Henry just ditched me! Do you even realize that? You called me, like, four times in January! That's it! And it was only to talk about HIM."

"You had no right. No right at all!"

"I just wanted everything to go back to the way it was before."

" . . . "

"And I didn't realize you liked him so much, not . . . like that. And it happened before I knew you were moving to Japan! Before watching you mope in bed for three days straight! I swear, Franny, you have to believe me. It happened before you told me you were moving."

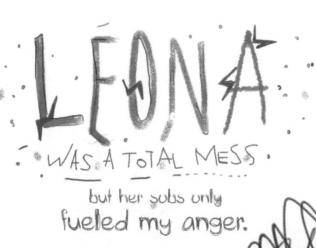

LEONA

WAS A TOTAL MESS.

but her sobs only
fueled my anger.

"Omigod, Leona, that's not a reason! And why are you telling me all this now?! What do you think it's going to change?! I'm on the other side of the world! It's a thousand times too late!"

"I know, I just . . . I mean, I tried to tell Henry, but . . ."

"But, what? What did he say? Go on, spit it out."

"He said . . ."

"Please just tell me."

"He doesn't believe me. He thinks I'm lying to protect you."

"You're disgusting, Leona Gingras."

"Don't say that."

"I don't want to have anything more to do with you, ever again. Or him. Or anyone else."

"Please don't hang up, Franny. I don't want to lose you."

I stared hard at Leona, unblinking, before slamming my laptop shut. I spent the next minute picturing her all alone in her room, sitting next to my empty bed, wallowing in the silence, in her massive pile of guilt. In that exact moment, I realized Leona had inadvertently taught me a valuable life lesson:

the truth
rarely hides far behind

the lie.

And the truth that took root inside me—and what I couldn't help thinking—the second I checked out on my best friend sounds an awful lot like this: you've already lost me.

I JUST CAN'T BELIEVE SHE DID THAT.

APRIL

Too many secrets are just as bad as too few.

Exactly a week to the day.

Last Thursday, right after her tidal wave of confessions—and even though I'd been very clear when I hung up on her—my former best (and only) friend tried calling me at least 75 million times. I couldn't believe it: Leona even had the nerve to call my father. I don't know what came over me, but after that happened, I made him the world's rashest promise:

"Dad, I'll tell you everything that happened,
if you promise not to answer. I don't want to talk to her,
and I don't want you talking to her either."

Then—*bam!*—just like that, without thinking twice, I spilled my guts to my father. To my great surprise, he listened in silence, without interrupting me even once. I have to admit, I've never seen my father so upset. He could barely get his words out straight.

"Are you sure, I mean completely sure, you understood her correctly, Franny? Leona can't have done everything you say she did . . ."
"Yes, Dad."
"Jeez. I don't know what to say, sweetheart."
"That's okay. You don't need to say anything."
"We'll cancel the party at Yoko's mother's. We'll postpone to next Saturday, sweetheart."
"For real?"

"Give me a little credit, Franny! Do you think I'm incapable of putting myself in your shoes?"

"Well, let's just say it's not normally your specialty."

"You've just gone through something terrible. Let's take some time to sort it out."

In the moment, it felt good knowing my father was on my side for once. Well, almost: I realized I'd said too much when he walked away from his Kraft Mac & Cheese preparations to pick up the conversation I'd (incorrectly) presumed was over. As I was pretending to read the ingredients on the side of the pasta box, he sat down next to me.

Like a lot of people born in the 1970s, my father considers anything salty and fattening to be comfort food . . .

Awkward.

"Stink bug . . ."

"What?"

"The Sam in question, the one you . . . kissed . . ."

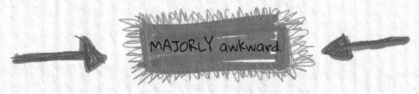

MAJORLY awkward.

"Dad, do you know how many boxes of Kraft Mac & Cheese are sold every week around the world?"

"Don't change the subject, Franny . . . Was it THE Sam?"

"Seven million."

"All right, that's what I thought. You kissed my colleague's son."

"Every week, Dad! All over the world! That's a lot of macaroni and cheese."

"Okay. No need to panic. It was only the one time, it's not a disaster, it might never happen again. Right, Franny? You aren't thinking of . . . doing it again, are you?"

"Omigod, Dad! I never should have said anything to you. I'm so stupid sometimes!"

"No, no, you were right to trust me, sweetheart. I just need you to understand that if Dimitri stops funding my research, it will kind of mean . . . the end of my work here. The end of my . . . career. That's all I'm trying to say. That's all."

"Dad, I don't want anything more to do with Sam. Anyway, he's not the kind of guy who stays interested in a girl like me for very long."

"What do you mean by that?"

"I'm five feet, two inches tall, I have plain brown hair, I weigh 95 pounds soaking wet, and my boobs aren't even big enough for a real bra."

I know. Cringe.
I had a "girl talk"
with my father.

"You're the spitting image of your mother. And she was the most beautiful woman in the world. So, if Sam can't see that, then it's his loss."

"Dad, I don't plan on dating Sam, and the chances of Henry forgiving me are about as good as us reversing the effects of climate change. Okay? SO CHILL OUT."

But my father looked only half relieved. And yet, I meant exactly what I said. Sam and I are already

O
V
E
R

(at least, I think so).

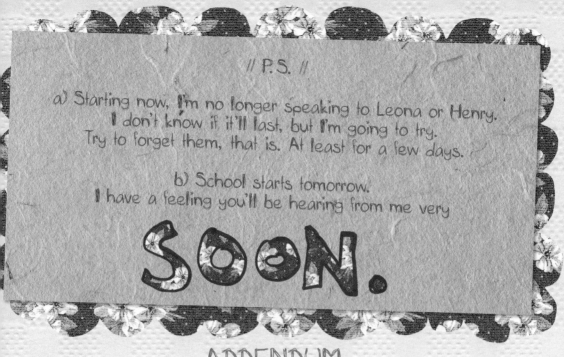

// P.S. //

a) Starting now, I'm no longer speaking to Leona or Henry.
I don't know if it'll last, but I'm going to try.
Try to forget them, that is. At least for a few days.

b) School starts tomorrow.
I have a feeling you'll be hearing from me very

SOON.

ADDENDUM:
FASHION DISASTER

I didn't expect to be writing another entry TONIGHT, Diary, but my father, true to form—that is, full of nasty surprises—just walked into my room with a big bag full of clothes. At first, I wasn't sure what was going on, but by the time he'd tripped over a few of the awkward sentences that have become his trademark, I realized I was expected to wear a uniform at my new school.

A UNIFORM!!!!!!!!!
BLECH. GROSS. VOMIT.

On top of that, guess who had the brilliant idea to order every single item in size large because, and I quote:

"Too big is better than too small, stink bug . . ."

Lame.

My skirt hangs down to my knees, I look like an astronaut in my gray pants, and my chest looks even flatter than a pancake under the massive white blouse that my dopey father chose for me with absolutely zero care. (grrrrrrr)

IT'S EXACTLY (YES, EXACTLY) AT TIMES LIKE THIS THAT I THINK HAVING A MOTHER WOULD SOLVE AT LEAST 50% OF MY PROBLEMS.

My father doesn't understand ANYTHING about fashion, ANYTHING about girls, ANYTHING about my entire existence.

Monday, April 3
8:33 p.m.

Hope in the form of ground beef with pizza sauce

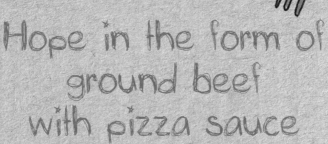

I couldn't resist stealing the menu off the cafeteria wall at lunchtime today, after I failed to choke down the unidentifiable, gelatinous, greenish—and possibly inedible—contents of my plate. So, it looks like I'll be making my lunches EVERY DAY from now on. There's no way I'm eating "ground beef with pizza sauce" or "bacon-fried cheese." Gross!

Ohhhh no.

You have to wonder who wrote this menu. Clearly, someone who speaks English as well as I speak Japanese :)

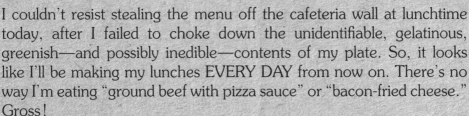

1月 献立表			April menu		
1月9日		アラビアータスパゲティー Spaghetti arrabiata	ワッフル Waffle	ゼリー Jellied fruit	
1月10日		サンドイッチ Sandwitch			
1月11日		鮭のムニエルレモンバター Grilled salmon lemon butter	ポテトサラダ Potato salad	ハムカツ Breaded ham	チーズカリカリ揚げ Fried cheese
1月		チキンソテートマトバジルソース Chicken stir fry tomato basil sauce	マカロニケチャップ煮 Ketchup macaroni	いんげんとベーコンサラダ Bacon bean salad	とうもろこし Corn
		ハッシュドビーフ Beef stew	プリン Caramel pudding		
1月16日	月	サーモングラタンカツ Breaded salmon au gratin	イタリアンスパゲティー Italian spaghetti	ブロッコリーサラダ Broccoli salad	小松菜ソテー Stir-fried komatsuna
1月17日	火	サンドイッチ Sandwitch			
1月18日	水	MIXグリル Mixte grill	キャベツのツナサラダ Tuna coleslaw	ジャーマンポテト German potatoes	コーンソテー Stir-fried corn
1月19日		フライドチキン Grilled chicken	豆サラダ Pee salad	コロッケ Nugget	むし枝豆 Steamed soybeans
1月		ミートスパゲティー Spaghettis bolonese	クッキー Cookies		
1月	土				
1月	日				
1月23日	月	エビカツオーロラソース Breaded shrimp aurora sauce	ミートボール Meat ball	人参と枝豆サラダ Carrot and soy salad	さんま芋のレモン煮 Lemon sweet potatoes
1月24日	火	サンドイッチ Sandwitch			
1月25日		黒り焼きチキン Chicken teriyaki	カリフラワーのマリネ Pickled cauliflower	MIXビーンズトマト煮 Mixte pees with tomato sauce	コールスローサラダ Coleslaw salad
1月26日		ベーコンチーズサンドフライ Bacon-fried cheese	かにかまサラダ Crab egg salad	南瓜レーズン Squash with raisins	ウインナー Sausage
1月27日		カツカレー Pork chop curry	エクレア Chocolate cream puff		
1月28日					
1月29日	日				
1月30日	月	ハンバーグピザソース Ground beef with pizza sauce	根菜胡麻マヨサラダ Vegetable salad mayonnaise sauce	カレーコンソメポテト Curry potatoes	豚肉の野菜巻き Vegetable wrapped pork
1月31日	火	サンドイッチ Sandwitch			

But let's start at the very beginning. My father insisted on driving me to school this morning in his latest purchase:

A "FADED JEANS" BLUE BEETLE

CIRCA 1969

FULL OF RUST

I could tell from the way he was gripping the vintage steering wheel that it was taking every ounce of self-control for him not to mention the Sam thing. I could also tell he would have given the moon and all the stars for me to reassure him, for me to say, just before walking into my new school:

"I promise, Dad, I won't do anything to mess up your career as an inventor, and my romantic adventures in my new life in Japan will be just as dull and uninteresting as the shade of blue on your new Beetle, okay?"

But instead of telling him what he wanted to hear, I babbled on until his little rust bucket came to a stop outside my new school:

"Dad, I think I know why you love your new car so much."
"Why is that, sweetheart?"
"Because it's as creaky as a rickety old boat."
"What? Our car is perfect. Open the glove compartment."
"Why?"
"Go on, open it, you'll see!"
". . ."

— A LICORICE DISPENSER —

My father had turned the glove compartment into a . . . licorice dispenser. When I was eight, I would have squealed, "Wow, Dad! So cool!" But at fifteen, all I could think was, *Right, so THIS is what you do all day while I'm stuck at school?*

"What do you think, stink bug?"
"Um, well, it's . . . special. Really great. We definitely wouldn't starve if we ever broke down in the desert. Okay, gotta go!"
"Oh, by the way, there's a lasagna in the freezer, in case I get home a little late tonight . . ."

"Seriously, again? You missed dinner last night too."

"I know. I'll try my best to finish early, but Dimitri is pressuring me to—"

"Dimitri this, Dimitri that. Sometimes I think you should date him instead of Yoko."

I opened the car door and stepped out without so much as a goodbye.

"I love you, sweetheart."

"Me too. Anyway, what choice do I have? You're all I have left. I don't even have Albert anymore."

"Franny, don't say that. And Albert's . . . . fine. Don't worry."

"You talked to Lorette? Never mind, I don't even want to know. I don't want anything to do with them anymore."

"If you say so."

" . . . "

"Good luck, stink bug. Call me if you need anything."

Good Luck.
Whatever.

Clearly, my father has forgotten what it's like to be a teenager: it wasn't luck I needed to survive my first day at a new school, it was a

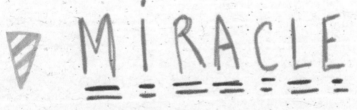

MIRACLE

(or, at the VERY least, a uniform that FIT.)

To make sure the odds were in my favor, I decided to get to school an hour early this morning, thinking those sixty minutes might give me an edge over the other students—kind of like a cat marking its territory, you know? Anyway, it made sense to me at the time.

But, apparently, I wasn't the only one with the same idea. Which I realized as soon as I stepped into the lobby. Perched on a ladder was a tall red-headed girl who was obviously struggling to hang a banner from the ceiling.

Welcome to Kyoto French Secondary School

Totally pretentious name, by the way.

"Hey, you! Can you give me a hand?"

OH No, NoT HER.

It was none other than Ms. Fashion Plate herself a.k.a. Capucine, right there, less than ten feet away from me. Of all people, I had to end up face-to-face with her, on the first second of the first minute of my first day of school.

I even thought:
Franny Cloutier, there's no question about it,
you must have done something terrible in a former life
to deserve all this bad luck.

Caught completely off guard but determined not to let this chick get the best of me a second time, I walked away from her and her weird contortions, thinking, *Oh man! If this girl thinks I'm going to be at her beck and call, she can take her manicure and her perfect hair and go jump in a lake!*

I heard her call after me:

"Thanks, new girl! Much appreciated!"

But I ignored her. I hoisted my too-heavy backpack full of too-new books onto my shoulder and began my search for room **09-A**. When I walked into my classroom two minutes later, I realized something had just happened.

Something strange
and inexplicable.

Diary, no word of a lie, Capucine was sprawled out, half asleep, across her desk at the very back of the classroom. I thought to myself: impossible. **Thirty seconds** ago, she was standing on top of a ladder, completely upright, as alert as someone who's just downed six espressos.

"Good morning, young lady."

My teacher.
A woman whose impeccable outfit
was matched only by her flawless face.

"Hello."
"And your name is?"
"Um, Franny. Franny Cloutier."
"Cloutier, is that Belgian?"
"No, I'm from Montreal."
"Ah! Well, you're very punctual in Quebec!"

"Choose a desk, but please be quiet, girls. I have a million things to finish up before the others get here."

{FAT CHANCE} OF ME TALKING TO HER.

"All right. Thank you."
"And kindly roll down your skirt. It's shorter than permitted."
"Oh. All right."

I sat down in the back row, on the complete opposite side of the classroom, pulling down my size-large skirt (but not too much) as I went. Without even bothering to lift her head, Capucine mumbled:

"You know they make that thing in your size, right?"
". . ."
"The skirt. They make it in your size."
"Get lost, okay."
"Oh, I see you haven't lost your Quebec charm."
". . ."
"What? Cat got your tongue?"

I felt like answering: "Are you kidding me? You were in the lobby THIRTY seconds ago! You bet the cat's got my tongue," but instead I kept my mouth shut and spent the next hour staring at the clock while Capucine flipped through a fashion magazine. When the bell rang and the other students poured into the classroom, I finally realized that I hadn't been hallucinating. That I'd actually made a

HUGE

HUGE
MISTAKE

LEFT ←→ RIGHT

LEFT ←→ RIGHT

mirrortwins

Forget a double take.
I had to look at least
ten times before it finally
clicked: same features,
same height, same
beyond-perfect
delicate beauty.

The girl that had just
walked into the
classroom
was a carbon copy
of Capucine.

Her twin.
It had to be.
Oh.

NO. CRAP.

OMG, Franny Cloutier, you've apparently become the world champion of putting your foot in your mouth! I didn't have time to agonize over it any longer, because my survival instinct was screaming at me to find a way to apologize to this girl, and fast.

Just then, Capucine no. 2 walked toward me—without so much as glancing at me—and sat at the desk right in front of mine. As I was subtly contemplating her thick red hair (and my despair at being such a loser), Sam and Leif walked in.

PHEW. HOPE.

Sam spotted me and came to sit down RIGHT next to me. I thought: *wow, even in a gray uniform, he's still cute.*

"Hi, Franny!"
"Hey, Sam! So, this is cool!"
"What?"
"That we're in the same class. You, me, and Leif!"
"Sure, it's cool, but it's only normal . . . there's only one Year 4 class here."
"Really? Is that all?"
"Yup!"

Then Sam leaned in toward me, like he was about to tell me a secret.

OMG.
Please don't let him bring up the party.
Please .... please.

"Hey, Franny."
"Yeah?"
"I hope you're not . . . mad."
"Mad? Why would I be mad?"
"That I didn't call you, you know, after the other night . . . I wasn't really sure what to, um . . ."

OMG.
He's bringing up the party.

"No, not at all. I swear. Anyway, I had a crazy week. It would take forever to explain, but honestly, I had no energy to think about anything else."
"Oh . . . okay . . ."

215

Wow.
How very
"Ms. Independent" of you, Franny.

I didn't have time to soften the blow, because just then, Capucine no. 2 turned around to look at us, obviously wondering what Sam and I had spent the last three minutes whispering about, and all I could think was . . .

Oh no.
Don't tell me these two
are friends.

"Francine, meet Franny. Franny, Francine."

No such luck.
She and Sam are, in fact, friends. Crap.
Good luck with your new life, Franny.

"Oh, hey . . . hi."
" . . . "
"Omigod, I just realized! Francine . . . Franny . . . we could be name twins!

BIG FAIL
on the witty comeback.

Francine just nodded her head. Meanwhile, Sam kept on whispering, only quieter.

"Don't worry. Francine is super sweet. She's just a little nervous because that's her mother up there."
"Wait, you mean our teacher is Capucine and Francine's mom?"

"Yup. Normally, she teaches the graduating class, but this year she's got the Year 4s. Francine is sure her mom is going to be on her case all year long, so she's freaking out."
"I bet! My God, I'd never want my father as a teacher. Poor her."
"Yup, poor *them*!"

So, you've already told off both your teacher's daughters. You've really outdone yourself this time, Franny.

Thankfully, the bell rang. Everyone sat down, and I was able to focus on something other than my social life. Ugh.

Ms. Clara—**that's what our teacher wants us to call her**—spent at least an hour explaining that she'd be our teacher for all our core subjects, except for gym, English, and Japanese. That's right . . . Japanese.

4 HOURS PER WEEK
And by the way, I checked: there's no getting out of it.

My God.
I already suck at math.
Now I'm going to suck at math AND Japanese.

Something I realized right away about Ms. Clara is that she's at least a thousand times nicer than her precious little Capucine. And she's definitely got a "type":

... but she's really
nice.

P.S.
All day long, I tried to find a way to talk to Francine, to convince her I wasn't as awful as I'd seemed this morning, but she was constantly busy! She's the head of some kind of welcoming committee for new students, and she basically spent the entire lunch hour being nice to everyone.

Apparently, I told off
Mother Teresa
this morning.

I really need to fix this tomorrow . . . you think?

Bye, Diary. And by the way, it's a good thing I have you. I know sometimes I try to act strong, but the truth is, I'm not really.

I can't keep my eyes open.
This jet lag is brutal.

Franny x

Tuesday, April 4
6:20 p.m.

Sushi
overdose

Dear Diary,

Do you think it's possible to overdose on sushi? I ask because my father just called again to say he won't be home for dinner tonight. Meaning, for the seventh time in two weeks (because Dad thinks it makes up for him not being here), I'll be eating the same thing:

SUSHI.

Before, I used to consider
sushi
a comfort food.

ONE MORE TINY PIECE
OF RAW FISH

INTO MY POOR,
CUTURE-SHOCKED BODY.

I REFUSE
TO
ADMIT

- WHAT IS HIS PROBLEM? -

I mean,
why was he so desperate for me to come live with him
if he's only going to spend
his entire life
working?

A Either my dad needs to chill out and start focusing on having a somewhat normal family life.

B Or he needs to find me a really patient cooking instructor to teach me how to survive here without dying of hunger.

By the way, he really should consider coming home. First of all, because I obviously don't deserve to be left alone in this tiny, depressing apartment every single night of my life, but mostly because I have something really big to tell him.

Something that won't
exactly
impress him.

SAM,
LEIF,
FRANCINE,
AND I,

will be cramping his not-quite-glamorous inventor's style
for the next six weeks.

222

LET ME EXPLAIN.

Today, Ms. Clara announced that 30% of our social science grade will be based on a big research project that we'll have to do in teams of four—and that we'll have to present in six weeks in front of the ENTIRE school.

According to Ms. Clara, she came up with the idea when she realized all her students at Kyoto French Secondary School had one thing in common: they've all been uprooted by their parents. Even though I wasn't too sure what she was getting at, I had to agree with her.

"If you're here, in this classroom, it's probably because your parents had to move here for work, correct? Maybe you've even moved more than once in the same year and had to make all new friends, start over again . . . not knowing whether or not you'd even stay! Am I right?"

Apparently, I wasn't the only one in this boat: all around me, I could see heads nodding in agreement. Ms. Clara sat down cross-legged on her desk, and I couldn't help thinking: total hippie.

"I'd like all the new students to stand up, please."

I hate it when they do this.

But when I saw at least half my classmates stand up, it gave me the courage to do the same. And it made me realize something: if there are any outsiders here, it's the students like Sam, Francine, and Capucine. The ones who stay. The rest of us all have something in common . . .

ALONE
LOST NEW

So, for once, I'm just:

NORMAL!

"But that doesn't mean you can't be happy here. Because it's—"

Just then, Capucine, still slumped over her desk, interrupted her mother, her voice dripping with arrogance: *What's with her, anyway? It's like she's always as tired as a 200-year-old lady!!!*

"Because it's our life. And our life is beautiful, and speeeeeecial."
"Thank you, Capucine. Especially for your sarcasm. I'm happy to see some of your lessons stick."

Capucine's attitude didn't faze our teacher one bit.

"Where was I? Oh, right. In teams of four, you'll write a research report on one of your parents and the work they do. Choose your teammates wisely, because for the next six weeks, you'll be working together in the field every Friday afternoon!"

Leif raised his hand:

"*Alors* . . . you're saying we'll have every Friday afternoon off?"
"That's not what I'm saying at all! Think of yourselves like interns, like your subject's shadows. You'll be detectives . . . investigating what drives them, what makes them happy. And during your sleuthing, I want you to keep this word in mind . . ."

Ms. Clara stood up and walked over to her brand-new, start-of-the-year chalkboard, where she scrawled—in giant capital letters:

"The goal of this research project, which I like to call "Roots," is to get you thinking about happiness, about why you're here, in this classroom, in this country, in this . . . life!"

blah ✔ blah blah Blah

At the time, I felt like Ms. Clara was a little over the top with her grand (and not-so-contagious) ambitions of happiness. But regardless, we had to form teams made up of new and old students, and that's how (yay!) Leif, Francine, Sam, and I all ended up together.

"We should do our project on your dad, Franny."
"Ugh, my dad? That's really not a good idea, Sam, trust me."
"Okay, but we can't choose my mother, she's our teacher, or Sam's father, because spending time with him would really suck."

"Oh, really? He's that bad?"

Francine's expression,
said it
all.

"Why don't we do it on your mom or dad, Leif?"

"*Ma mère* is a diplomat, and *Papa* just follows her around everywhere. It would be really boring, because everything she does is top secret."

"Okay, but my father repairs sewing machines for a living, so . . . are you sure you won't regret it?"

"No. Your father *used to* repair sewing machines. Now, he's trying to change the face of humanity."

"The face of—"

"Humanity, yup. Franny's father is trying to figure out how to stop aging, cancer, Alzheimer's disease, and a bunch of other heavy-duty stuff."

"Wow, that's big."

"Okay, it's decided. Franny's father."

"Fine . . . But don't say I didn't warn you!"

We made up our minds so quickly that we were able to spend the rest of the class swapping life stories.

// P.S. //
Francine never mentioned our run-in yesterday morning.
Phew!

The only thing I don't understand is what's going on (or no longer going on) between me and Sam. We did kiss at the party the other night, didn't we?

226

DID I DREAM IT?

Later, Diary,
I'll update you if there's anything new.
F. x

A coffee
for humanity

(At 6:58 a.m., Dad and I were already sitting
at the table eating our cereal.)

"Sweetheart, I don't know what to tell you. I don't think it'll be possible. Following me around like that, everywhere . . . Every Friday afternoon, you said?"
"Yup."
"For six weeks?"
"Yup."

Endless sip of coffee:
my father's way of
biding his time.

"I really doubt Dimitri will go for this. Actually, I'd be amazed if he did. I'll have to check with him . . ."
"Already done, Dad. Sam asked his father. He's fine with it."

"I need to hand in my research report at the end of the month, Franny. I can't afford to get sidetracked; things are already intense."

My father watched me swallow a huge spoonful of cereal. He knew that I knew (that he knew) that wasn't a valid point.

"Dad, give it up. You're not going to win this time. I'm doing my research project on you, and we'll be spending all our Friday afternoons together, and I want to know EVERYTHING about your life."
"Wow. I don't think I've ever seen you so determined."

As much as to say his arguments were useless against my iron will.

"You're always telling me to look on the bright side, Dad! So, maybe if I understood what you do, I could decide for myself whether or not it's worth it!"
"Whether what's worth it?"

"Duh! Japan!"

My father stared at me for three whole seconds. I could tell he was proud that I was taking a stand.

"Okay. Sold. But if you guys throw me off schedule, I'm kicking you all out, Franny."
"Deal."

I stood up so fast (proud of having won the battle, if not the war) that I took the tablecloth with me. So, not only did my father start his day off with a dose of bad news but he also ended up with scalding-hot coffee down the front of his favorite shirt.

"Oops. Sorry!"

Ooh. Really not impressed.

"Franny! Get back here!"
"Gotta go, I'm late! And the Japanese really frown on that!"
"Franny, you go to a FRENCH school!"
"Love you!"

Whatever. If my father's smart enough to save the human race, I'm sure he can manage to get a stain out of his shirt, right?

F. x

Thursday, April 6, 8:45 p.m.
(continued)

The French kiss theory

Based on my life over the past few months—chaotic and unpredictable—I'm forced to believe that everything's going a little too well here and that, statistically speaking, there's at least a 104% chance of things going sideways.

Proof that everything is going
too smoothly:

SUMMARY OF MY ARRIVAL HERE

1) After just four days of school,
I've already made three friends. THREE.

2) The hottest guy in school kissed me
(but is acting like it never happened. Weird, I know).

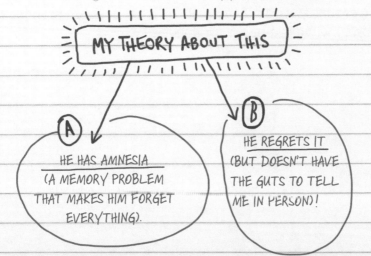

MY THEORY ABOUT THIS

A) HE HAS AMNESIA
(A MEMORY PROBLEM
THAT MAKES HIM FORGET
EVERYTHING).

B) HE REGRETS IT
(BUT DOESN'T HAVE
THE GUTS TO TELL
ME IN PERSON)!

3) Um . . . there is no number 3 right now.

Anyway, I obviously messed up badly today, and if everything blows up, I won't be able to blame my father (for once).

It all started when I tried to be nice to the meanest girl on the planet: Capucine. Even though Capucine is exactly the type of girl I have zero pity for, I actually felt really bad for her this morning, when she had to confess—in front of the entire class—that she hadn't found ANYONE to do her research project with. Needless to say, Capucine doesn't exactly have the best reputation in the world . . .

This came as no surprise.

What was surprising, however, is that Ms. Clara miscounted the number of students on her list! Once she realized there were actually 25 of us—and not 24—she told Capucine to pick a team to join.

And when I noticed all my classmates staring at the floor to avoid making eye contact with her, I just found it too . . . cruel, Diary. It reminded me of how alone I felt in the school bathroom in St. Lorette, and how I probably would have died of loneliness six months ago if Leona hadn't invited me home for spaghetti.

It reminded me of . . .

LEONA

"You can join us, Capucine."

Francine, who was sitting right next to me, gave me the least subtle kick in the history of the universe.

"What are you doing?! My sister is nuts!"

Not one to swallow her pride, Capucine kept me waiting like she had a thousand other options to consider. Please, girl. I didn't have all day.

"No one is forcing you, Capucine. I was only—"
"Okay. Yes. I'll join you."

Sam, Francine, and Leif probably want to kill me, but I know I scored major brownie points with Ms. Clara—you should have seen the way she looked at me for the rest of the day!

WE START TOMORROW.
AND I SWEAR: CAPUCINE HAD BETTER WATCH HERSELF.

I've heard people say that it's better to give than to receive.

I guess we'll see if that's true . . .
Franny x

The bike belonging to the old Japanese lady downstairs

Thanks to the 150-year-old lady who lives downstairs—you know, the Japanese woman who lives in that weird shop that sells lipsticks and powders—I won't have to ride to school anymore in that rusty, old blue contraption my father calls our "car."

When I went outside this morning after I got tired of waiting for my father—it takes him an eternity to get ready—I came face-to-face with the old lady. It's like she was waiting for me there, on the sidewalk, waiting to talk to me. She placed her hand on my arm and spoke to me in flawless but weirdly accented French.

"You may use this bicycle, little one. It was mine, but my legs are too old now for such nonsense."
"Seriously? Oh wow, thank you! But are you sure?"
"It's my pleasure, little one."
"My name is Franny."
"Maybe so, but I think here . . . we should call you Fubuki."
"Really? Well, I don't know, I don't speak Japanese. But you . . . you speak really good French for . . ."
"For an old Japanese lady?"

OOPS.

"Yeah, I guess."
"You should be more careful, you know."
"I know, I'm sorry, I really didn't mean to offend you."
"No, I'm talking about your shoes, little one."
". . ."
"It says a lot about a person, the way they treat their shoes."
"Well, it's just that . . . I happen to like them this way."

By the way, since my stupid argument with Sophie about our Nikes, I've only worn Converse.

I looked down at my shoes and couldn't help thinking: my old beige Converse are only becoming cooler with age. I love every one of the stains on my shoes. I even have a special fondness for the pieces of chewing gum stuck to the soles. But I couldn't blame this old Japanese lady for not understanding; her weird-looking sandals look like something straight out of another century!

When she noticed me looking at her feet, the grandmotherly old lady just smiled. I'd judged her right back, and I'd been caught in the act. In her raspy voice, she said one last thing before slipping back inside her shop.

まなかさんのくつ

MANAKA'S SHOES

"Well, if you like them, then your shoes are perfect just the way they are. And you can call me Manaka. Have a lovely day, little one. See you tomorrow!"
"Okay. Thank you . . . for the bike!"

Did she just say see you tomorrow?

Never mind.
Yay!
A bike.

P.S.
By the way, I'd love to take the bus or the subway, but since all the signs are in Japanese, it's probably not a good idea since I still can't remember the name of our neighborhood.

The bike might date from the late 19th century,
but at least it works!

FREEDOM,
HERE I COME!

The boat

"Franny? You're not at school? You kids either?"
"Daaad! Please tell me you haven't forgotten!"

When my father opened the door to his lab this afternoon, it was obvious that the five of us were the last thing he expected to see. And that our notepads, whirring tape recorder, and overdose of enthusiasm weren't exactly what he considered a pleasant surprise.

"Forgotten what?"

Sam obviously isn't the only
amnesiac
in my life.

"It's Friday, Dad. Our research project . . ."
"Good Lord, Franny! You only told me about it the day before yesterday! I didn't think you'd actually show up this week!"

I sighed for three whole seconds before turning to my teammates.

"I told you! My father is the biggest scatterbrain on the planet."

Sam tried (mostly unsuccessfully) to step up as leader of our little group:

"It's just that we have a pretty tight deadline, Mr. Cloutier. What if we just watch you work? We won't say a word. We'll sit at the back of your lab and won't make a peep. One hour, tops, and we're out of here! Would that be okay with you?"
"I'm very sorry, but you can't stay. Not today."

Seeing him about to close the door to his precious lab, I knew I was the only one capable of handling my pig-headed father.

"Dad, no."
"Franny, don't make me embarrass you in front of your friends."
"Don't make ME tell them how you ALWAYS put me second!"

With that, my father opened the door wide and replied tersely:

"I DO NOT put you second, I'm just doing my work!"

What happened next made me feel like I was in the middle of a real-life soap opera: from out of the blue, Yoko appeared, breathless and dressed like she was about to embark on a trek through the Amazon rainforest.

"Hubert, sorry my love, I'm late! Everybody's ready, the boat is set, they leave soon, so we better hurry."
". . ."

Noticing me standing there, she switched to her broken French:
"*Bonjour*, Funny, you here . . . Happy to see you. I tink it be long time we no see each other, you and me."

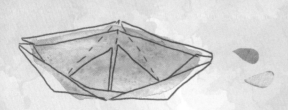
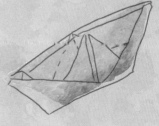

THE BOAT

I had no idea why she was there. But I suddenly understood why my father was so eager to get rid of me. He was planning to get on a boat, yet AGAIN, and he'd had the nerve to hide it from me, yet AGAIN.

"Come on, everyone, we're leaving."
"Sweetheart, wait."
"I don't think so. Save your breath to explain to your girlfriend that my name is actually FRAN-NY."

And I left. Obviously, knowing exactly how I felt about his news, my father didn't try to stop me. Leif, Francine, and Capucine followed me without a word, but Sam seemed too shocked to move.

"Franny, what are you thinking?!"

I was thinking, *Too bad for you, Sam, feel free to stay here.* I left my father's work—a big, gray, depressing building on a depressingly gray street that crisscrosses the entire east side of Kyoto.

I took off at warp speed on my rusty old bike, unintentionally leaving the others in my dust. But to be honest, I was glad to be alone.

At home, I ran into old Manaka—needless to say, I was completely out of breath, totally fed up, and in no mood to chitchat with a 150-year-old lady.

"Hello, little one. Oh my, what's happened?"
"Nothing. I have a lot of homework. I have to go inside."
"You look upset, Fubuki."
"Listen, what is it with you Japanese people not calling me by my name?! My name is Franny! Fran-ny!"

I stalked into the house, slamming the door behind me. It was the first time in my life I'd ever been rude to a person, shall we say, of a certain age. And weirdly enough, being mean to Manaka didn't feel as good as I'd thought it would. Neither did picturing her there, alone on the sidewalk, arms dangling next to her flowery dress, wondering if I am the exception or if everyone from Quebec is so badly raised.

I ran to my room, pulling off shoes and coat as I went, dove straight under my covers, and curled up into a little ball. All I could think was: if my father is fine with getting on a boat again, after everything that's happened, then it must mean he's willing to take the chance—however slim it might be—of abandoning me.

I know that thousands of people take thousands of boats every single day. But it's not every day a father risks turning his daughter into an orphan.

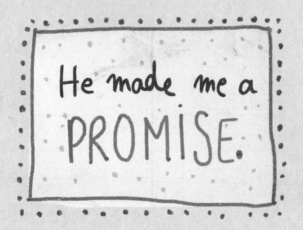

He made me a
PROMISE.

My phone rang at least 25 times tonight. I knew it was either my father or Leona, so I ignored it.

And I didn't order takeout sushi either.

F. x

Bye bye, bonsai

"Franny, wake up."
"No."
"Fine."

Whenever my father says *fine* after I've just defied him, that's definitely a bad sign. Something told me I'd better get out of bed, and fast. When I walked into the kitchen, I found him staring at his reflection in the oven window, fighting with the knot on his tie—my father has always sucked at tying a tie.

I helped him, even though my level of empathy for him was practically nonexistent.

I know it's weird, Diary,
but I actually know how to tie a tie.

- KNOTS -

- THE FIGURE 8 -

- THE WINDSOR -

- THE TREFOIL -

- THE HALF-HITCH -

- THE HALF WINDSOR -

- THE SHEET BEND -

"Why are you getting all dressed up like that? It's Saturday."
"I see I'm not the only forgetful one here."
"What are you talking about?"
"Breakfast at Yoko's mother's. In twenty minutes."
"Seriously?! Like, now?"
"Yes, seriously, Franny."
"I don't see why I should do everything you say when—"
"You know, I'm starting to think Yoko is right."
"Oh really, and what brilliant thing does Yoko have to say?"
"That I should be stricter with you."
"Oh, really?"
"For starters, you should understand that if I need to get on a boat for work, Franny . . . Hey, don't walk away from me! If my work . . ."

I turned on my heel and walked back to my room, leaving his sentence dangling as limply as his tie.

"Yoko needs to mind her own business."

He followed me, just to make sure I understood I was on HIS territory, in HIS house (classic move)—an attempt to act like, you know, a normal father.

"I want you downstairs in twenty minutes, Franny. I'm leaving now. It'll give you some time to think."
"Think about what?"
"About the kind of impression you want to make. And I'm warning you, don't even think about pulling that bikini stunt again."

My father turned to go, muttering something about my makeup.

"But downstairs where, exactly, Dad?"
"Yoko's mother lives on the main floor!"

I can't believe it.
The 150-year-old lady
with the weird sandals
is . . . Yoko's mother?

12 MINUTES

later, I'd thrown on a cute yellow dress just decent
enough not to completely embarrass my father.

Whatever,
it's not like he deserved it.
Not even a little bit.

"Hello? Is anyone home?"

No one answered when I knocked at old Manaka's door, so I let myself
in. I could tell right away I was inside an authentic Japanese home; it
was nothing like our shabby apartment. Two words: *minimalist* and
Zen. Everything was put away so neatly, so perfectly, that I almost
didn't dare breathe. I took off my shoes and walked down the hall to
the main part of the house . . .

So far,
so good.

I knew the guests were at the back of the house—probably in the dining room—but it was the odd space (like a store, but not quite) at the front of the house that caught my eye. I should have told myself, "Franny, stop it. This isn't your house. This isn't even your country. Go straight to the dining room!" But instead, I stepped inside the room that had . . . caught my eye.

One word:
dummy.

It was obvious I was standing in a shop. The walls were plastered with photographs of geishas, and it smelled like incense, or something like it. Tall shelves were lined with tiny pots of cream and powder and lipsticks that had been meticulously sorted and that, at first glance, all looked identical. A bunch of foreign newspaper articles were pinned to the back wall. As I took a step closer to read them, a headline jumped out at me from an old issue of *Paris Match*.

"Manaka Osaki, owner of the oldest authentic beauty-product shop for geishas."

MADAM MANAKA

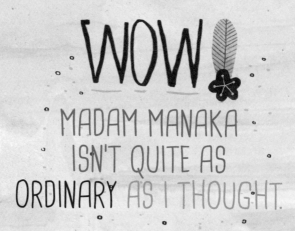

WOW!

MADAM MANAKA ISN'T QUITE AS ORDINARY AS I THOUGHT.

That was the exact—yes, exact—moment I should have left the shop and gone to join my father, who must have been seriously starting to wonder why I was taking my sweet time. But instead, I walked over to a miniature tree under a glass case.

BAD IDEA (n° 1)

I swear, Diary, I was only trying to figure out what made the little tree so special that it deserved all that attention. Which is why I tried to open the glass door.

BAD IDEA (n°2)

But it was stuck, and I must have tugged a little too hard, because the entire thing crashed to the floor.

I stood there for a full minute, staring at the tiny, defenseless tree that I'd just murdered. I tried to convince myself it was just a little pile of dirt at my feet, no big deal, but deep down, I knew it was proof of a sad but true fact:

EVERYTHING YOU TOUCH, FRANNY CLOUTIER, TURNS INTO A DISASTER.

Why does my life always have to be so complicated? Why can't I just be like everyone else? Why? Why? Why?

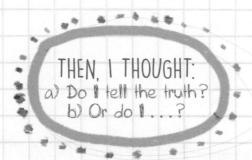

THEN, I THOUGHT:
a) Do I tell the truth?
b) Or do I . . .?

I had no other choice, and I knew it. Anyway, the truth always comes out, which is something I now know for sure. So, head down, I walked to the dining room, planning to confess everything—to my father, at least.

To be honest, Diary, I didn't quite realize what I'd just broken, otherwise I might have SERIOUSLY considered option B. But it's a moot point now, because as I write these lines, it's obviously a thousand times too late.

So.

In the doorway to the dining room, I took a massive deep breath (for courage). I noticed my father notice me. And because he knows me like the back of his hand, he knew—from the look on my face—that something had just happened.

"Franny, come over here, sweetheart. I want to introduce you to Mr. Osaki, Yoko's uncle."
"No, you come here! Please. It's, like, kind of urgent . . ."

My father excused himself to the man in Japanese and walked over to me.

"Pretty dress."
"Dad, I, um . . ."
"Franny, you're as white as a sheet! What's wrong?"
"Well, it's just that . . . I think I broke a tree."
"A tree?"
" . . ."
"Sweetheart, you can't just 'break' a tree."
"Well, it was a . . . mini tree."
"Oh no, Franny!"

My father followed me to Madam Manaka's shop.

He was walking behind me,
but I could hear his breathing
becoming more and more ragged.

Inside the shop, once he realized what had happened, my father literally dropped to his knees and started trying to pick up the remains of the half-uprooted tiny tree. I heard him muttering something about his life savings and how we would be ruined.

When I knelt down beside him—I was only trying to help, Diary—I swear he screamed at me with all the air in his lungs:

DON'T YOU DARE TOUCH ANYTHING!

My father's scream echoed all the way down the hall, turning our family secret very public. A minute later, the entire Osaki family was standing in the shop, staring down at my mess. Obviously, Yoko and old Manaka were there, but at least they kept their mouths shut—unlike the others, who made no bones about whispering in Japanese and staring at me like I'd just assassinated their prime minister. I didn't know what to do, Diary.

"Dad, please don't be mad. I'll buy them another tree. I promise."

My father turned toward me very slowly, like in a Western movie when the bad guy is getting ready to draw his gun, a move calculated to drive home the seriousness, the gravity, of my botanical botch-up.

"It's not a tree, Franny. It's a bonsai. A 390-year-old bonsai! Yoko's family has been tending it for generations. This bonsai survived the bombing of Hiroshima! And it was Yoko's inheritance!"

". . ."

"Do you realize what you've done? Do you even realize?! It was priceless, Franny. Price-less!"

Everyone looked on as all my tears and my last remaining shred of dignity streamed out of my body. I felt completely and totally worthless, that's right,

so, to stop my father from humiliating me any further, I screamed at the top of my lungs.

"Then why did they leave it here all alone?!"
"Franny, get upstairs."
". . ."
"Now!"
"If you hadn't forced me to move here, none of this would have happened! It's your fault my life is ruined! I hate you!"

My father looked up at me then, and I swear, Diary, he's never looked at me like that before. His sense of calm was scary, his anger wrapped up tight in a silence I couldn't break through because of the huge lump in my throat. That's when I understood the show was over.

"Franny, upstairs."

I walked out without looking back. I dried my remaining tears as I dragged myself up the stairs on legs that felt like they weighed five hundred pounds (each).

But when I raised my head, I saw someone, sitting cross-legged, in front of our apartment door.

SAM

"Franny, we need to talk. I found out some cool stuff about your father yesterday. You should have stayed at his lab. You'll never believe it. Your father is planning to—"
"He'll kill you if he finds you here. Believe me. Go home."
"Hey, what's wrong with you?"
"Just go, please."
"Can't you just tell me what's wrong . . ."

I shook my head, indicating to Sam that it was pointless. But he was like a dog with a bone.

"Franny, I can't leave you like this."
"Please go. I need to be alone. Anyway, I only destroy everything I touch."

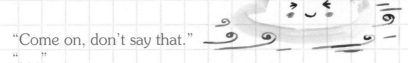

"Come on, don't say that."

" . . . "

"What you did, Franny . . . for Capucine, well, no one else would have done it. Believe me."

"Well, believe me, I'll only end up hurting you, so just get out of here."

"Maybe I'm . . . willing to take that risk."

Sam traced a finger under my eye to catch the tear running down my cheek.

I thought to myself: maybe I'm not completely
alone in the world
after all.

I googled it earlier: Hiroshima is a city in Japan that got hit with an atomic bomb on August 6, 1945, at the end of World War II. All kinds of people died and lots more got cancer (because of the radiation). So sad.

Through my shame—and shame doesn't even begin to scratch the surface of how I was feeling—I told him about Madam Manaka's 390-year-old bonsai. He listened right to the very end, and I cried right to the very end, stopping only because even pain exhausts itself eventually.

"Franny?"

"What?"

"The bonsai . . ."

"What about it?"

"I'm thinking . . . if it was tough enough to survive Hiroshima, it just might be tough enough to survive Franny Cloutier, don't you think?"

I smiled.

Even though I know full well that
words
can never fix everything.

"Why are you always so nice to me, Sam?"
"I don't know. I feel good when I'm with you. That's all."
"Hey, Sam."
"What?"
"Could you . . . I mean, would you mind . . ."
". . ."
"Holding me . . . in your arms?"

Sam took a step forward. I let him wrap his arms around me, comfort me. And if I could have disappeared completely in his arms, dissolved into a thousand pieces, and left my own body, I think I would have.

I tilted my head back a tiny bit, just to see. See into the depths of his eyes.

What on earth could make him
want
the pile of misery I've become?

I inched my face closer to his and stared at his lips, like actors do in the movies, just before they kiss. I always thought they did that to line themselves up properly with their costar's face, but it actually felt natural. I wasn't trying to imitate a movie star. I wasn't thinking about aiming for anything. I didn't care if it was less than perfect.

And that's how it happened. For the second time, and despite the mascara running down my face, we kissed.

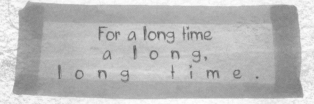

For a long time
a   l o n g,
l o n g   t i m e .

Just long enough for me to realize that . . .

I FELT GOOD and EMPTY AT THE SAME TIME.

EVERYWHERE and nowhere AT ONCE.

I swear, Diary, I wish I could have been stronger, but the truth is, even as I was kissing Sam, I couldn't help thinking about Henry. About the last few times we'd seen each other. About the last nights we stayed up talking while everyone slept. About him trying to spread jam on my toast in the dark. Just the right amount of jam.

Even though I know that's all
6,312 miles away now ...
I still couldn't help wondering:

Is this Henry's legacy, this emptiness I feel?
Am I doomed for the rest of my life
to kiss only half-heartedly,
to live only half a life?

And what if we only get one love,
one true love?

What if the heart
just gives out
after that?

NO.
I refuse to believe

THAT.

*It won't happen, Franny.
Each time you get close to Sam,
Henry will not find a way to
invade your brain.*

I made that pact with myself and when I opened my eyes, I could breathe better, better than I had in months. I made Sam promise not to suffer from amnesia anymore or to forget our latest kiss, and he swore he'd still remember it on his 88th birthday. That was more than I'd asked for, but I just said: okay.

***

He eventually left, and my father came home. We didn't speak to each other the entire day. In fact, the only time I heard my father talk was to Yoko, who knocked on our door, to check in, I guess. I wasn't brave enough see her. I spent the day drawing and writing to you, and now I'm going to bed.

This day is finally over, and I'm sure I'll remember it for the rest of my life as the day I got over my first heartbreak, right after murdering a 390-year-old bonsai.

Good night, Diary,
F.

Wednesday, April 12
9:23 p.m.

I am a
snowstorm.

I promise I'll tell you how it went at school post-French kiss with Sam in the stairway, but NOT BEFORE I tell you this one little thing.

I just spent the evening at Manaka's house. She and I had dinner together. My dad got home from work super early today, but I decided making him eat alone might force him to realize how badly it SUCKS to spend the evening by yourself, watching TV and eating takeout sushi. Anyway, my father has been like a broken record since Sunday; whenever he says anything to me, it's all about how I can "best" make it up to Manaka.

Strategies proposed by my father:
1. Clean Manaka's house every Sunday (fat chance).
2. Work in her shop a few hours per week (meh ...).
3. Give her something meaningful (?).

Strategy or no strategy, after thinking about it for **72 HOURS**, I knew it was high time I worked up the courage to apologize to Yoko's mother for destroying her bonsai. I'd prepared a very long, very elaborate speech, but in the end, these are the only words that came out of my mouth the second she opened the door:

264

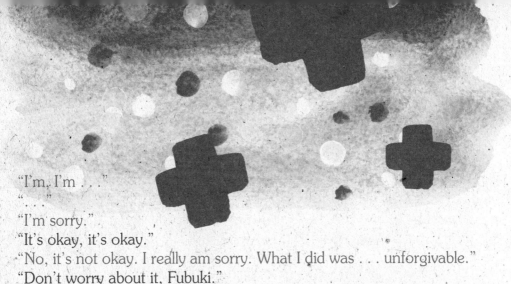

"I'm, I'm . . ."

" . . . "

"I'm sorry."

"It's okay, it's okay."

"No, it's not okay. I really am sorry. What I did was . . . unforgivable."

"Don't worry about it, Fubuki."

" . . . "

"Perhaps that bonsai ended up on your path for a reason."

"Yeah, to make my life more complicated."

"It's all a matter of perspective."

"But it was your inheritance, Manaka. And Yoko's too. And that bonsai survived the fallout from an atomic bomb. My father even told me your family nicknamed it 'the Survivor.' You have every right to be mad at me until the end of time."

"Oh! Until the end of time—that would be far too exhausting. Plus, I've sent it off to the hospital. Good people, near Hiroshima, are taking care of it as we speak."

"The hospital? You have bonsai doctors in Japan?"

"You could call them that, yes."

"That's pretty funny."

"You're right, it is. You know, if you're feeling up to it, you could come to Hiroshima with me to pick it up once it's healed."

"Yes, I'd be happy to. You can count on me, Manaka."

Whew. I can't tell you how relieved I felt, Diary, knowing Manaka had forgiven me. She sat down next to the window, which I took as an invitation, so I did the same—but I didn't touch anything, I swear. I sat there looking at her, without saying a word. But mostly without a clue.

Most people are super attached to their possessions, obsessed with the value of things. But Manaka seems to be above all that. I mean, she barely knows me, but already she's . . . . forgiven me?

> What if forgiveness
> had the power to change us
> for the better?

We spent the next hour talking about anything and everything except for butchered bonsai. I found out that the reason Madam Manaka knows how to speak French (and Greek and Mandarin and English and Italian!) is because she's spent her whole life studying philosophy.

"But I don't get it, Manaka. You need to speak a whole bunch of languages to study philosophy?"
"No, not necessarily, but I felt it was important to understand the subtle meanings of the authors' words."
"Why?"
"Well, because certain words carry their own special significance in each language."
"That's weird, my mother thought the same thing. She loved Italian."
"Then she had excellent taste!"
"*Il dolce far niente*, does that . . . does that mean anything to you, Manaka?"

I don't know if that expression only makes sense in Italian, but it made Manaka giggle.
It only reminded me . . . of Leona.

And then I wondered whether, like Manaka, I'd ever have the strength to forgive Leo for what she did to me. I mean, it wasn't some 390-year-old bonsai she ruined.

It was my first real love.

"Manaka, can I ask you one more question?"
"Yes."
"Why do you always call me Fubuki?"
"Snowstorm."
"What?"

Manaka stood up and left the room. When she came back, she was holding a sort of paintbrush. She dipped it into a pot of ink and began tracing letters on a sheet of rice paper.

フブキ
fubuki

SNOWSTORM

"The first time I saw you, I could tell you've been carrying it deep inside you, since you were a little girl."
"Carrying what?"
"That snowstorm, in your heart."

Manaka held out the paper to me. I hesitated for a moment before taking it from her, then I looked her straight in the eyes.

"You know, I wasn't like this, before my father moved here."
"You really believe that?"
"I may have broken your tree, but you don't know anything about me, Manaka."
"All right."
"No, it's not all right. You don't know anything."

I stood up.
I had come,
I had apologized,
and I had even been forgiven.

But I was in no mood to hear that I'd be as unsettled as a snowstorm for the rest of my life. I was about to leave the room when Manaka, eyes downcast, asked me one last question.

"Do you know the main reason why most people end up drowning?"

I turned to face her, speechless, paralyzed. I replied curtly—because drowning isn't exactly my favorite subject:

"No, actually, I don't know."
"Fear."
". . ."

"They thrash around in a panic, run out of strength, and slip beneath the water."

"Okay. But why exactly are you telling me this?"
"Because that's what you've been doing, ever since your father moved to Japan. You're afraid, and you're thrashing around in all directions. If you really must know, that's why I call you Fubuki."

I stared out the window next to Manaka for a long, long moment. I wished she'd yell at me instead, call me anything other than that, other than a snowstorm. But I knew, deep down inside, she was right.

"You could transform all that energy into something very beautiful, little one."

"I have to go now, Manaka. My father will be worried. Good night."

"Good night, little one."

"Are you just going to stay here? You're not going to lock the door?"

"No. I'm old, and, well, it's not like anyone can steal my bonsai just at the moment."

"Yeah . . . right. Well, good night."

I need to go tell Dad about my evening with Manaka. I promise I'll write when I get home from school tomorrow (about Sam, I mean).

Franny (or Fubuki?) xxxx

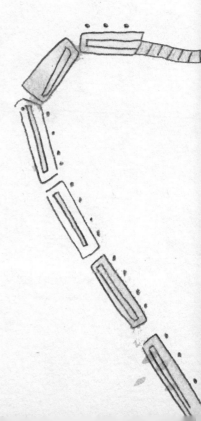

In love
on two continents?

I got my period this morning. I'm telling you because I always feel sad or happy or annoyed when I'm menstruating. I can't help it. By the way, I always wonder whether that word is just as ugly in every other language.

Menstruating. Gross, admit it.

Anyway. Period or no period, the news I got at 7:42 this morning would have been just as shocking in any other situation

imaginable.

So, as I was saying, at exactly 7:42 a.m., as I was hopping on my bike to go to school like every other morning since I've been in Japan, I heard my father call out to me.

UP
I looked ↑↑↑ and saw his head poking out the tiny window at the front of our apartment.

"Franny, come back up here, please. There's someone on the phone for you."

"Really, Dad?! I'll be late for school!"

"Franny, it's important."

"If it's Leona, I don't want—"

"It's not Leona. I'll drive you to school. Just come up here."

I got off my bike, wondering what could be so URGENT that my father would be willing to make me (possibly) late for school. As I climbed the stairs, I decided it might not be such a bad idea to get there after everyone else this morning. Because things at school have become pretty complicated over the past three days. Let's just say when Capucine saw Sam slip his hand into mine on Monday morning, she got the shock of her life.

SO DID I, BY THE WAY.

I mean, yes, I'd made Sam promise to remember our kiss. And yes, I would have been upset if he'd forgotten—again. And yes, I like him, a lot (maybe even more than that), but I never dreamed we'd come out openly as a couple.

A REAL COUPLE?

Even writing it feels weird.
Not a good sign.

Anyway. I'll get back to that later because what happened next is a thousand times more important. When I walked into the kitchen, my father handed me his phone and stepped away—not like him to care about my privacy, I thought.

"Seriously, who is it?"
"I'll be in the living room, Franny."

I looked at the call display: unknown number.

"Hello?"
"Franny, it's, um . . ."
"Henry?"
"Yeah."

We spent the next minute listening to each other say nothing. I was waiting for Henry to speak, to say something, anything! Waiting because I knew if I went first, I would say the wrong thing.

And the truth is, that empty space between us was better than the silence of the past few months.

"It's Albert, Franny."
"What about him? What's wrong?"

"He died, this morning."

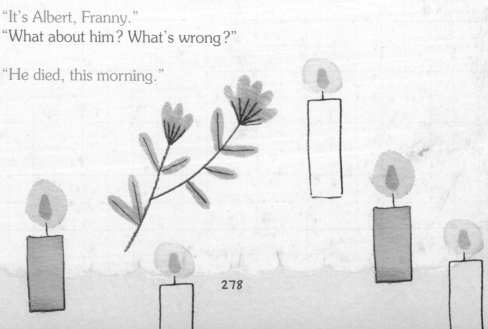

278

I lost it. I must've screamed NO at least twenty times. Then I cried. A lot. And Henry just listened to me. Powerless to take away my pain.

You might not understand, Diary, but Albert was really important to me. My dad gave him to me for my fourth birthday, right after my mom died, because he didn't know what else to say or do to ease my pain. And it worked: Albert made me feel better all those times in my life I needed comforting.

But this time, he would have needed me, and I was here, and I'm sure he died of a broken heart, all alone in his cage.

"Where is he now?"
". . ."
"Where is he? I want to know."
"I put him in a . . . shoebox . . . outside."
"Are you crazy? He'll be eaten by some animal!"
"I know. My dad said we're going to take him to the vet. I'm just waiting for him to get home from work. We'll have him . . . cremated."
"Ugh! With a bunch of cats and dogs. No way."
"Franny . . ."
"NO WAY."
"Okay, okay, I'll think of something."

I knew I could rely on Henry,
and it calmed me down,
in the moment.

I barely remember
anything after that, Diary.

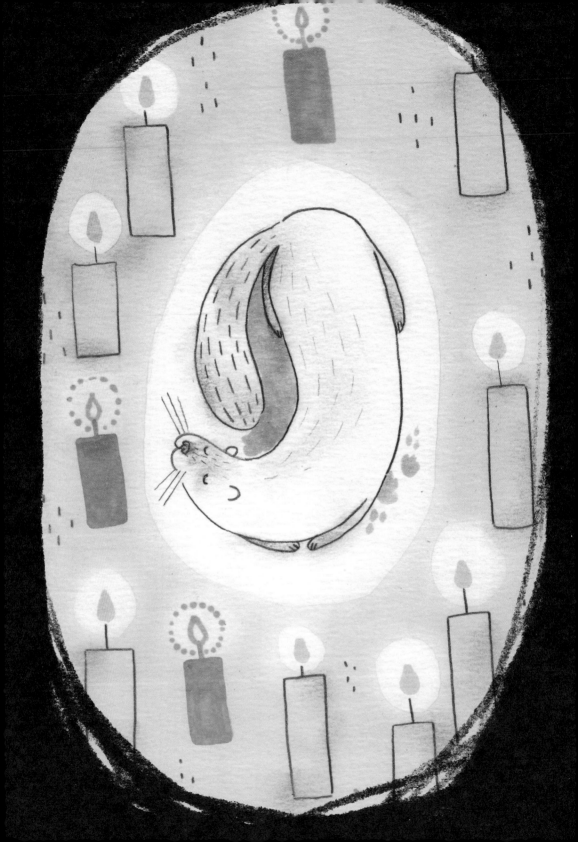

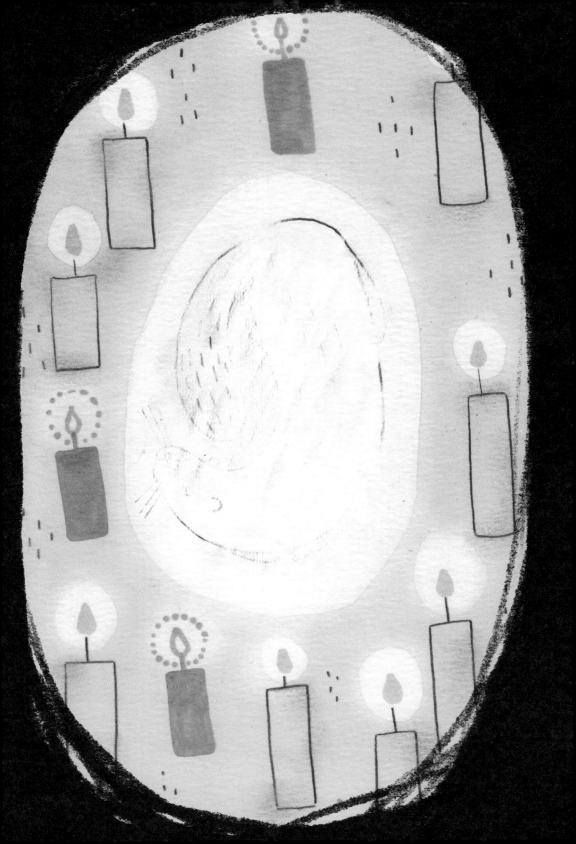

I also knew we had nothing more to say,
but without really knowing why,
I stayed on the line

all the same.

"Franny, I know this probably isn't a good time, but . . ."

". . ."

"Is it true, everything Leona's saying? She tries to tell me at least five hundred times a day that . . . well, that everything that happened is all her fault."

"You're right, Henry, it's not a good time."

I've been waiting for this moment for months
and now it's here,
and honestly, I don't even know if it's what I want
anymore, Diary.

"Sorry. I shouldn't have brought it up. Bad timing."

". . ."

"I'm sorry about Albert. I really cared about him too, you know."

"Uh-huh. Bye, Henry."

"Bye, Franny."

I stood frozen in the middle of the kitchen, staring at my father's phone in silence. And even though the news of

Albert's death was taking up
99.9999 %
of my available head space,

I couldn't help wondering if there was even the tiniest chance that Henry believed me, but more than that, what it might change if he did. I mean, it's impossible to be in love with two guys on two different continents, right?

Don't even think about it, Franny Cloutier.

Good night, Diary. Good night, Albert. Good night . . . Henry.

F. x

Saturday, April 14, 1:55 a.m.
(sleepless night ahead)

The ocean, my father, and me

There's no way I could

EVER
sleep with everything running through my mind tonight, Diary.

1. Albert ... I just can't stop thinking about him.
2. Capucine hates me (officially), and I think she's cooking up a very uncool plan to make me pay for dating Sam (also officially).
3. You'll never believe me, but I spent the afternoon on a boat. I swear.

You're probably wondering whether I've spoken to Henry again since our conversation on Thursday morning. The answer is:

no.

And honestly, I plan to avoid talking to him for as long as possible. Because I know the first thing he'll ask the next time we talk is *How are things going in Japan?*

And then I'd have to tell him about me and Sam. And then it would just be . . . over.

Over for good,
between Henry and me.

And I really have no idea what I want. Like, REALLY no clue. And that's the truth. I mean, I'd finally managed to get Henry out of my head! And Sam is the best thing that's happened to me since I moved to Kyoto! I hope you don't think I'm pathetic, Diary, but on Thursday, during geography class, I made two lists—you know, to help me decide.

SAM ♡

- Super sweet
- Has never hurt me
- Hottest guy who will ever be into me, for the rest of my life
- Really, really good kisser
- Lives in Japan
- Moving a little too fast
- Speaking of too fast, I don't think I'm ready for my first time (with him?)

HENRY ♡

- My first love ♥
- Hurt me (in fact, I've never been so devastated in my entire life)
- Cute
- Lives in St. Lorette
- Knows everything about me
- No chance of moving too fast in a long-distance relationship
- I can't stand his mother

Let's just say, I got to school this morning more confused than ever.

I was in the middle of emptying out my entire locker because I'd lost my Japanese textbook yet again (apparently, my subconscious refuses to learn the language) when I felt two arms wrap around my waist. I don't really know why, but I froze. I couldn't even turn around.

"Hey, you." *OMG, why can't I ever just act like a normal person?*
"Sam?"
"Well, yeah . . . Were you hoping for someone else?"

I confess, in that moment, I thought, Henry?

But to chase away the tsunami of guilt that washed over me, I did what all couples on the planet do, I imagine, and moved in closer to Sam to kiss him. At that exact moment, the locker door right next to mine slammed (brutally) shut.

CAPUCINE

If I could have sunk through the floor, Diary, believe me, I would have.

Sam stared at Capucine for a long moment, then he turned back toward me. Very slowly, he leaned into my neck and started kissing me softly. Well. Let's just say, before this morning, no one had ever made a move on me like that, Diary. But you know what?

NOT ONLY WAS IT *perfect* . . .

IT WAS TOO PERFECT.

I mean, the massive aura of perfection that follows Sam everywhere he goes, in everything he does, makes me feel like a complete and total loser. The LAST thing I am is perfect! Especially when it comes to making out. As you know, Diary, I'm so terrified of doing it wrong—putting my tongue in the wrong place, turning it the wrong way (is there a right way?), acting too relaxed or not relaxed enough—that I seriously don't even know WHAT I'm doing.

Quite frankly, I find French kissing completely exhausting.

So, I can't say I managed to fully enjoy the feeling of Sam's face nestled in my neck—and anyway, I could tell his move was completely calculated, designed to let Capucine know she was wasting her time.

"I plan to be with Frammy whether you like it OR NOT."

The look Capucine gave me just before stalking off made me feel like human garbage. At the same time, Sam was gazing at me like I was the eighth wonder of the world. That was the exact moment I truly understood the meaning of the word *paradox*.

Six minutes (and a huge hickey) later, the second bell rang. That's when we realized we were late. Sam grabbed my hand, and we started running through the hallways. I kept dropping my books because he was making me laugh so hard, and that's pretty much the state we were in when we spilled into our classroom, only to come face-to-face with Ms. Clara.

"Whoa! Settle down, you two! Is this what Friday does to you? Take your seats! You know I don't tolerate late arrivals."

Judging from her almost indulgent reaction to our over-the-top entrance, I knew my asking Capucine to join our social science team had won her over forever. Ugh, but if she knew how much I hated her daughter, I think she'd revoke my teacher's pet status on the spot!

By the way, she's the first teacher who hasn't found me annoying, and I admit, I kind of like the feeling.

Sam finally let go of my hand. I quickly settled into my seat, and Ms. Clara went on teaching:

My Japanese teacher, by the way.

"Mr. Konoki called this morning to say he'd be late, so I wanted to make sure you've all decided on your social science project. How's everything going so far?"

Capucine raised her hand.

"Yes, Capucine?"

"Well, I'm sorry to tell you, we haven't started yet, because Franny forgot to warn her father last Friday. And I really wouldn't be surprised if she forgot to tell him about this afternoon either. Let's just say she's a little distracted these days . . . Isn't that right, Franny?"

Francine turned to look at me.

"What did I tell you? My sister is crazy."

Ms. Clara was obviously disappointed.

"So much for being loyal to your teammates, Capucine. But, Franny, I'm sure I don't need to tell you that your entire team will suffer if you don't take this project seriously."

I was about to offer up a bunch of excuses—it's true, with the news of Albert dying and everything else, I'd forgotten to warn my father YET AGAIN—but Sam beat me to it: phew

"Actually, Capucine, if you'd been paying attention, you'd know we're meeting Franny's father at 2 o'clock this afternoon. He's invited us to observe a group of bowhead whales. Franny's father studies them because they're the longest-living mammals on the planet. Two hundred years, apparently."

Ms. Clara turned to me.

"That's very impressive, Franny!"

Even though I had absolutely NO IDEA
what Sam was talking about, I went along with it:

"Um, yeah . . . I know, yeah, he's into some really crazy stuff . . . my dad."

Capucine shot daggers at me. Whatever. The only person she managed to humiliate today was

By the way, I've decided to stop calling her Cappuccino (I really don't need any more bad karma).

HERSELF.

But humiliated or not, she still ended up on the boat this afternoon with Leif, Francine, Sam, and me. That's right, you heard correctly, Diary. I got on a boat today.

And it all
started
during our Japanese class.

— Notes passed —
between Sam and I
during Japanese class this morning:

Hey! What's this about the whales? Some kind of joke?
No one knows what you're talking about, Sam!!!
(Thank you, by the way.)

o˙ʍ

It's actually why I came to see you last Saturday, but we ended up doing . . . other things.
:)

Ha ha. Very funny.
Stop fooling around,
Mr. Konoki's going to catch us!!

Okay . . .
So, after you all left last Friday,
I stayed behind.
Your father had just canceled his boat trip.
He seemed really disappointed, by the way.
After Yoko left, he gave me a tour of his lab!

Okay . . .
But he's never said anything about whales, only jellyfish . . .
You must have misunderstood.

No, so what your dad has discovered is that (basically), some jellyfish have the same ability as bowhead whales to fight off cancer and live a super long time! Essentially, he's trying to find the link between the two species!

Yeah, Turritopsis jellyfish,
they actually age in reverse
= become young again.
YOU SEE! I do know some things about my father :)
But what's the deal with the boat?? And why was Yoko there?

Yoko works for an organization
that fights against whale hunting.
She's invited your dad to go see them for the first time and it's
happening . . .
this afternoon.
And we're INVITED!!!!

What?!! But why did you keep this a secret all week?
You could have told us sooner, it's in ONE HOUR.

I know, but it's because
your dad told me about
how you . . . get seasick.

Seasick????

He told me there was no way
you'd want to come.
That you get seasick on boats.
I thought if I waited
to tell you, you might come . . .
I just didn't want you to miss it.

Um, pretty lame strategy, Sam.
Anyway, you can tell me all about it later.
I can't go . . . there's no way I'm getting on any boat.

????

Chill out with your question marks.
Forget it, I'm not going.

Seriously, your father is trying to figure out
how to cure a bunch of diseases
and help people live longer,
and you're not interested?! Like, you'd rather
stay behind, all alone in Kyoto?

Yup, 10-4, you got it.
I think I'll do some sightseeing. I've barely seen
anything since I got here.

Franny, you don't need to be
embarrassed. If you need me
to, I'll even hold your hair
while you puke.

DID YOU NOT HEAR ME?
I said I wasn't getting on any freaking boat.
AND STOP TALKING ABOUT MY DAD LIKE HE'S SOME
KIND OF HERO.
IT'S — GETTING — ON — MY — NERVES.

After reading my last note—written in huge capital letters—Sam
turned to face Mr. Konoki, listening raptly to everything he had to say
(in Japanese) about the different ice-cream flavors available in Japan.
As soon as class was over, Francine, Leif, and Capucine gathered
around Sam's desk because, very clearly, he was the only person who
had a clue.

"Sam, what exactly is going on?"

"What's going on is Franny is staying behind. Whoever wants to can follow me, but we need to leave right now. I'll tell you everything on the way there."

"Wow, I bet you two wouldn't last more than a month, but an hour? That's . . . wow . . ."

"Shut up, Capucine."

"I'm coming with you, Sam."

"Me too."

"We'll fill you in on Monday, Franny . . . Bye."

I watched them go off, knowing there was nothing I could do to stop them. Sam didn't look back even once, and that's when it hit me: I'd just cut myself off from everyone.

AGAIN.

And it made me think about that thing Manaka had said,
about people who drown.
Maybe she was right
after all?

I stood up and yelled as loudly as I could:

It took ages for him to come back to the classroom, but at least he did.

"I told you my mother died . . . Well, it was a boating accident. I didn't tell you how it happened, because . . . because I'm just so sick and tired of talking about it! So, that's why I'm so . . . scared."
"But, Franny, if you'd told me that to begin with, I would have never insisted—"
"I want to come."
"Are you sure?"
"Yes."

BUS RIDE CONFIDENCES

Apart from Capucine, everyone seemed happy to see me. I sat next to Francine on the bus, and we talked nonstop the entire way. And I realized it was the first time we'd talked one-on-one since we'd met. And you know what? I think I missed talking to another girl. I mean . . . a girl my age.

At one point, we fell silent, and Francine stared out the window at the passing scenery. I'm not quite sure why, but I pulled out my sketchbook and started drawing her face, turned toward the window.

"What are you doing?"
"Nothing, just drawing."
"Can I see?"

I hesitated. Because apart from my underwear drawer and my diary, my sketchbook is probably the most private thing in my life.

"Um, okay."

I held it out to Francine and started gnawing on the eraser at the end of my pencil, one of the silly things I do when I'm nervous.

"Hey, is this me?"
"Um, yeah."

"It's really good."
"You think?"
"Really. Is this your diary?"
"No, it's just a regular notebook. I mean, I have one, a real diary. I even draw in it sometimes, but . . . ugh! It's hard to explain."
"I have one too—a diary."
"Oh, yeah?"
"Yup. But I don't know how to draw."
"Oh. Well, I could teach you, if you want."
"Okay."

I let Francine look at my drawings.
All my drawings.

It felt really weird. I'd never shown them to anyone before. Not even Leona.

No,
not even Leona.

Francine thinks there's something special about my drawings and that I should believe in myself more. I felt shy when she said that. I mean, I don't draw for other people—and especially not because I have any big ambitions. I draw because I think there are just some things you can't describe with words. But I didn't know how to explain that to her, so I just changed the subject.

"I really don't get how your sister can be so crazy!"

"   "

"I mean, you're so nice. And Capucine is the complete opposite."

Francine turned to look at her sister, like she wanted to make sure her twin wasn't listening. Capucine was wearing giant headphones, and we could hear Adele blaring from the front of the bus, but Francine still lowered her voice to a whisper.

"My sister has never been very good at making friends."

"Yeah, let's just say . . . I noticed."

"No, I mean, she was like that even when we were little."

Francine hesitated before going on. I could tell she was wondering if she could trust me.

"She'd kill me if she heard me telling you this, because she really doesn't want anyone finding out. Sam knows, but that's it. It's kind of like a family pact . . ."

"Francine, slow down, I don't know what you mean."

"My sister has epilepsy."

"What?"

"Yeah, and I think that's partly why she's, like, angry all the time."

"Epi-what? Is that some kind of disease?"

"Yeah, it's a neurological condition that makes life complicated for her and for our parents—they worry all the time."

"   "

"Capucine has to take medication every day, at exactly the same time, or she gets really bad seizures."

"Omigod."

"Yeah, you can't even imagine what it's like, Franny."

"What about . . . you? You don't have it?"

"No, I don't have it."

Francine lowered her eyes.

"Sometimes . . . when I was little, I wished I could be sick too. Just so my parents would worry about me. So they'd come check on me in bed at night, so they'd forbid me from going biking alone or text me nonstop like they do with my sister."

"I'm sure you just wanted to . . ."

"Feel like I existed, I guess. I don't know."

Francine's eyes filled with tears. I'm not exactly sure why I did it, but I laid my hand on top of hers.

"Poor you."

" . . . "

"This might sound harsh, Francine, but I don't think that gives her the right to act this way."

"Yeah, I know. But ever since her breakup with Sam, things have . . . gotten worse. I think she was less mean, before. But I don't know anymore."

Things were getting awkward, so I pulled my hand back and didn't say any more, even though I was obviously waiting for the rest of the story.

"When Sam first moved to Japan about two years ago, it was love at first sight for Capucine, and she became really sweet, like a better version of herself . . . They were together for five months."

"Okay. Then what happened?"

"Capucine got super jealous, for no reason."

"Of who?"

"Of me."

"But why?"

"I have no idea, I swear! Sam and I have always got along really well, but my sister couldn't stand us being friends, and eventually Sam couldn't take her jealousy anymore and he broke up with her."

"And she took it really badly."

"Exactly. She's never gotten over it, and she turned into the person she is now."

"Like, mean?"

"Yeah, you could say that."

I looked over at Capucine, like it might help me understand her better.

In the end,
maybe the people who find fault with
everything around them . . .

are just ordinary people
with a few scars on their
heart.

"Hey, Francine."

"What?"

"If you're interested in Sam, I want you to tell me, okay? I mean, I would never date him if—"

"Franny, my sister did it with Sam. No way I'd be into him after that! We're just friends. That is possible, right?"

GOOD QUESTION:
CAN A BOY AND A GIRL EVER TRULY BE JUST FRIENDS?

By the way, I knew what Francine meant
by "my sister did it with Sam,"
but I just wanted to be, like, crystal clear:

"So, when you say she 'did it' . . ."
"You know, the two of them, they . . . Oh, maybe I shouldn't have told you. It's just that everyone at school found out, so . . ."
"No, that's cool, I . . . I'd rather know."

OMG. I really wish I didn't know! Now, I have an excellent reason to freak out over Sam moving way too fast. Okay. Let's change the subject, because this reminds me way too much of my father and how he's always saying I *skip steps* (whatever). For once, I have to admit that the status quo in my fledgling love life suits me just fine.

So, there you have it. One hour—and a pile of secrets—later, the five of us arrived in Osaka, a city about thirty miles from school, on Osaka Bay, which empties into the Pacific Ocean and has a phenomenal number of bowhead whales.

OSAKA

When he saw me coming, I thought my father—whom Sam had arranged to meet at the front gates of the port—was going to have a heart attack.

"Franny? What are you doing here? Sam, didn't you tell her we were going on—"
"Yes, Dad, he told me."
"And you . . . I mean, you're coming?"
"Yes, Dad."
" . . . "

"Well, don't make that face, you look like you're about to have a heart attack."
" . . . "

"Oh man, are you crying? Stop, you're embarrassing me."
"Franny, this . . . this is the best birthday present you could ever give me, stink bug."
"Birthday present? Oh, crap. It's your birthday . . ."

I SYSTEMATICALLY FORGET

MY FATHER'S BIRTHDAY,
year in and year out.

306

*Omigod. Just writing it . . .
I can't believe I did that today.*

The good news is, for once I won't have to make it up to him by buying him a really awesome present. He was so thrilled I'd be going on his ocean expedition that he started babbling about his research with a passion that never existed back when he was a sewing machine repairman in Montreal.

And, I must admit, my embarrassment at seeing my father burst into tears on the dock in Osaka gave way to a huge dose of pride when I finally understood the reason for his dedication over the past few months. I mean . . .

I don't know if my father is really
the hero Sam thinks he is,
but at least

he's trying to do something
good, for humanity.

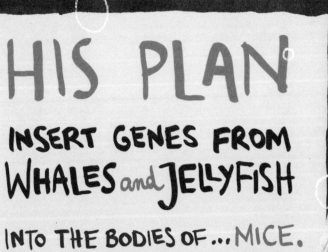

HIS PLAN

INSERT GENES FROM WHALES and JELLYFISH

INTO THE BODIES OF ... MICE.

So, To sum up what I learned today, my father is what they call self-taught: he learned everything, did everything, completely on his own. How? Basically, he absorbed an incredible amount of information from going to tons of conferences and reading tons of books about the longest-living animals on the planet.

"But, Dad . . . you're not going to, like, torture mice, are you?"
"Of course not, Franny! No, if everything goes well, I'll be running the research center that Dimitri and I plan to open next year. We're going to call it the Foundation for the Elimination of Aging!"
"Mm-hmm. Awesome name, Dad."
"I know! It was Dimitri's idea. Anyway, I want you to know, Sam, if it weren't for your father, none of what I've told you would be possible."

I turned to look at Sam. He was smiling, and I could tell he liked hearing about how his father had done something good too.

Just then, Yoko appeared on the dock to ask if we were ready to leave. And that's how, without overthinking it too much, I found myself aboard the:

*Mizu ga jōshō suru to, bōto wa,
onaji koto o yarimashita.*

Translation:
"When the water rises, so does the boat."

When I mentioned to Yoko that I thought it was a very, very long name for a boat, she explained that her organization felt it was important to choose a name that, like, actually meant something.

310

"We want make all whale fishers know whales stronger than they, you see, Funny?"

"Yes, I think so. Like, make them understand the whales will . . . adapt, right?"

"Yes, exact! Like you and Japan, maybe, Funny!"

"Yeah, we'll see."

". . ."

"It's really cool what you do, Yoko. For the whales, but also for my dad . . ."

As I was saying that, the boat pulled away from the dock. I closed my eyes and squeezed Sam's hand so hard it turned white. But he kept his promise and didn't let go, even though numb fingers are never fun.

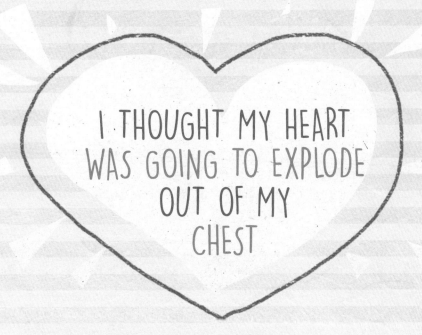

I THOUGHT MY HEART WAS GOING TO EXPLODE OUT OF MY CHEST

when we slipped out of the bay and a huge whale leaped out of the water less than fifty feet away from us.

I'll never forget how I felt that afternoon,
out on the water.

Part of me started to breathe,
for the first time.

And it was a day Capucine won't ever forget either! She spent the ENTIRE hour puking over the railing and having her back rubbed by Leif—ugh, poor him, I don't think he saw a single whale. But Francine filmed the whole thing and took at least 250,000 photos, so no worries.

By the way, it's official:

Even as she was hurling her lunch into the ocean, she found the energy to give me a look that could only mean *I'll get you, Franny.* I'm not even kidding.

But more importantly, I think, is that my father and I came to some sort of understanding today, about our lives. We'll never forget my mother, but we're going to try to . . .

The Horizon

WHEN I SAW THE WAY
MY FATHER LOOKED AT YOKO,

I REALIZED
SHE WAS PART
OF HIS HORIZON,
RIGHT NOW.

AND MINE,
BY EXTENSION.

But she loves whales,
so how bad can she really be?

When I think about it, I don't think I'll ever be as wise as old Manaka. But I know one thing for sure: by facing up to my greatest fear today, I was able to get just enough distance from that huge storm raging inside me to get a whiff of the air my mother loved so much.

The ocean air.

P.S.
Pizza night at Sam's house tomorrow. Everyone will be there. :)) Even my father. It's fine this one time, but I made Sam PROMISE not to start inviting him everywhere. I mean, just because my father is attempting to save the human race doesn't mean he has to become the third wheel in my social life.

Oh, yeah, and we're going to spend the day together tomorrow, just me and Sam.
Apparently, he wants to show me his favorite spot in Kyoto.

I KNOW what you're thinking, Diary. I need to tell Henry.

I know, okay?

F. x

(Mini) freakout in a (sacred) temple

"Franny, are you okay?"

"Sure, why?"

"I don't know, I just get the feeling you're embarrassed to hold my hand in public. Am I wrong?"

When Sam asked me that this afternoon, in the middle of the oldest temple in Kyoto, it took everything in me not to answer:

"Yes, you're wrong!
Why would I be embarrassed?
We're on the opposite side of the city, in the middle of a massive temple!
Surrounded by millions of tourists with zero chance I'll run into
THE only person likely to be upset by the fact that MY hand is in YOUR hand,
namely... HENRY!"

But instead of telling the whole truth and nothing but the truth, here's what I said:

"You really want to know?"
"Yes."
"Okay. Well, I know you DID IT with Capucine, okay? I know. And I don't think I'm ready. If you really must know, just the thought of making out freaks me out, and I don't know if I'll ever be ready. Um, I mean, obviously, one day, but right now I'm just too . . . confused! And you're forcing me to talk about it, which is making me feel even more uncomfortable, so that's why I always let go of your hand, if you really must know."
"Wow. That was a lot."
"I know."
" . . . "
"Everyone's staring at us, Sam. I think I was a little loud."

Sam just smiled at me. Without a word, he took a step forward and kissed me. ON THE CHEEK, Diary. I honestly don't think he could have done anything cuter! Omigod, this guy is just too perfect—what did I tell you?

But instead of calming me down or making me happy—I mean, Sam had clearly just let me know I had nothing to worry about and he basically wasn't expecting ANYTHING from me—his kiss on the cheek only made me feel a thousand times guiltier for continuing to hide my still-not-officially-over-based-on-recent-developments relation- ship with Henry.

I took a huge deep breath, and just as I was about to tell him everything, for better or for worse, Sam took a step back and said:

"Follow me."

ARGGG!

I stood frozen in place, thinking something like,
Dear universe, would you please give me a chance to act
like a decent human being for once!

But since Sam had already wandered off into some sort of weird, shadowy Buddhist forest, I had no choice but to put my "honesty is the best policy" plans on hold and follow him.

And that's how, 454 stairs later, I found myself on a lookout with Sam—and the worst dizzy spell of my entire life. And even though I'd never seen anything so spectacularly beautiful, naturally I managed to find the perfect way to ruin it:

"Hmmm. So, is this where you bring all the girls you date?"

Sam walked silently to the edge of the lookout. He stared straight ahead, hands in his pockets. Even though I knew I'd just said something hurtful, ruined the moment, my freaking pride kept me glued to the spot, twenty feet away from him.

"I don't know what you think, Franny, but I've only had one girlfriend since moving to Japan, okay?"

" . . . "

"And if you really want to know, we always went to her favorite place. I never brought her here because I normally always come to this temple alone."

319

"I'm sorry."

"Seriously, why are you always so nervous around me? It's over with Capucine! The past is in the past. You're the one I want to be with now."

"I know . . . It's not you."

I walked over to him and laid my head against his chest. I could hear his heart beating, racing. He pulled his hands out of his pockets and wrapped his arms around me, a sign we'd made peace with each other. After that, he started acting like some kind of weird tour guide.

Sam explained that the place where we were—the Temple of the Golden Pavilion—was first built in the 14th century but was burned to the ground by a very angry monk in the 1950s.

Apparently, when the people of Kyoto rebuilt it, they decided to cover it in gold leaf.

Sam thinks it was a symbolic way of showing the entire world . . .

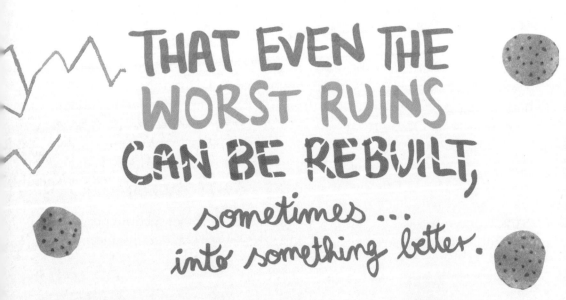

THAT EVEN THE WORST RUINS CAN BE REBUILT, sometimes... into something better.

I left the temple today with a huge question on my mind, Diary:

Basically,
what if it's not Sam I don't trust,
but myself?
And what I want,
truly want.

I'M GOING TO
END THINGS
ONCE AND FOR ALL
WITH HENRY.

And I'm going to do it
right after I finish writing these lines.

I might not know much about love, Diary,
but I know one thing for sure:
if I don't find the courage to talk to Henry,

nothing,
no part of me,
will ever be rebuilt (for the better).

Later!
(Wish me luck.)
F. x

TEXT THREAD

April 15, 9:10 p.m. Kyoto time
April 15, 8:10 a.m. Quebec time

Franny

Hey.

Henry

Hey.

Franny

I'm not sure I should be writing to you.

Henry

I was going to text you.

Henry

Albert was cremated.
All alone . . . I kept the ashes.
I did what had to be done. At least I think so.

Franny

Okay. Thanks.
. . . I mean it, thank you.

Henry

No problem.

Franny

Am I bothering you?

Henry

No, not really.

Franny

What are you up to?

Henry

Waxing my surfboard.

Franny

You surf? Really?

Henry

On the river. There's a wave,
but please don't tell your dad,
because then he'll tell my mom and she'll freak.

Franny

I won't, I promise.

Henry

Only my dad knows.
Like, I hide my surfboard at the bowling alley.

Franny

Relax, I won't say anything.

Henry

I believe you, Franny.

Franny Well, I hope so. I'd never say a word, I swear.

Henry No, I mean,
I believe that it wasn't you.
I read your letter.

Henry Why aren't
you saying anything?

Franny I'm just a little shocked,
that's all.

Franny I've been trying to
tell you that for months.

Henry I know.

Henry You're so far away . . .

Franny I know . . .

Henry I miss you.

Henry
You have nothing to say?

I had no idea if there was a "good" or a "less crappy" way of breaking the news to Henry, Diary, so I just blurted out . . .

Franny
I met someone.

Franny
Henry . . . say something, please.

Franny
Ugh, I knew you'd say nothing
and I'd just end up sitting here, staring at my phone,
like a big loser.

Franny
Whatever.
I guess silence is
our new thing.

Henry
What do you want me to say?

Henry
???

Franny
I don't know . . .

Franny

He's a good guy and he doesn't deserve to be lied to.

Franny

And neither do you :(

Henry

I gotta go. Tommy's waiting for me. Take care of yourself, Franny.
xxo

END OF TEXT THREAD

I won't say anything more because there's nothing else to say, and because my stress ball father (who can't even be bothered to get his own social life) is waiting for me at the door. Ugh, I can smell his cologne from my room.

"Franny! Stink bug! We're leaving. What are you doing?"

"Ugh! I'm texting someone, Dad! Can you just wait thirty seconds?"

"Hurry up, sweetheart, or we'll be late. Who are you talking to, anyway?"

"I'm talking to . . . Leona, okay? Besides, it's none of your business. You were invited to MY party, so chill out!"

He can be so annoying
sometimes.

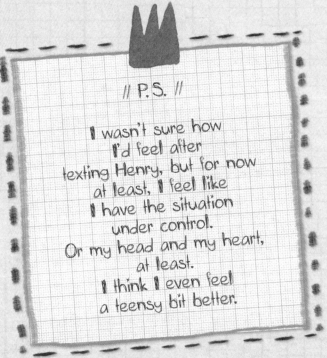

// P.S. //

I wasn't sure how
I'd feel after
texting Henry, but for now
at least, I feel like
I have the situation
under control.
Or my head and my heart,
at least.
I think I even feel
a teensy bit better.

I'm going over to Sam's for pizza night.
I might write again later tonight, Diary.

F. x

A downer
ending to the night

"I'm so ashamed you're my sister."

I'm pretty sure those were the last words that were said last night right before Sam's father kicked us all out of his office, then his basement, and finally his house. And, obviously, those words came from Francine.

To make a long story short, let's just say last night's pizza party ended the same way it began: as a huge downer. And this time, there's no chance—you got that, Diary?—**NO CHANCE** of me having even an ounce of pity for Capucine.

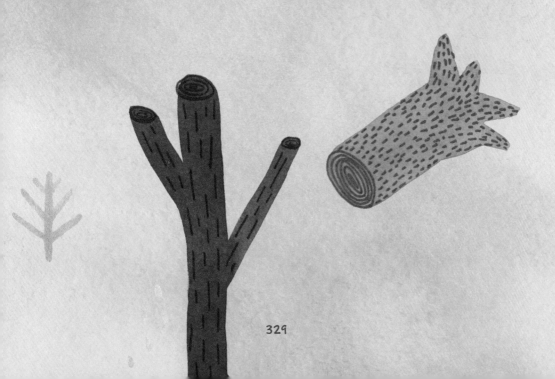

The second my father and I set foot in Sam's house, I could tell something was off.

"Hey, Sam! What . . . you can't even say hello?"
"Everyone's already here. The pizza's getting cold. Hubert, can I take your coat?"
"What about my coat? Hey, Sam . . . I'm talking to you."

It could not have been more obvious: I'd just spent an amazingly perfect afternoon with Sam, then when I saw him two hours later, he was avoiding me like 356 pimples had suddenly popped out on my forehead.

Clearly,
someone had said or done
something.

I grabbed Sam's hand just as he was about to disappear into the dining room. I pulled him into the kitchen, refusing to wait one second longer to talk to him. I lowered my voice to a whisper, even though public spectacles don't scare me one bit since the bonsai massacre.

"Sam, what on earth is going on?"
"Nothing, why? Do you know what's going on?"
"No, but you're being super cold. I mean, we had a great day together! Then I get here, and you're acting like a total jerk."
"I don't know what you're talking about, Franny."
"Stop messing with me, Sam!"
"Trust me, I would never. That's *your* specialty."

Sam dropped my hand, leaving me standing there, in the middle of the kitchen, with a pile of unanswered questions. He joined the others in the dining room, where he focused all his attention on Leif, who, fingers dripping with tomato sauce, was telling everyone about the history of the Margherita pizza—which, by the way, isn't worth repeating.

– THAT'S WHEN I (TOTALLY) LOST IT. –

When it finally dawned on me that Capucine had to be the reason for Sam's sudden and inexplicable anger toward me—even though I had no idea what she might have said to him—I stood up, obviously with no thought as to what I was about to say or do, and slammed both fists down on the table with all my might and screamed:

My father turned to face me, put down his slice of pizza like it was a ticking time bomb, and stood up too—clearly worried his career wouldn't survive a second diplomatic incident at Dimitri's house.

"Stink bug, I don't know what's happened, but calm down. Whatever it is, we'll fix it."

I didn't even bother to look at him. I just ran out of there, vowing to myself not to return until I knew THE ENTIRE TRUTH. Obviously, when Sam, Leif, and Francine saw me storm out of the dining room, they all followed me.

I stalked through the house, flinging open every door to every room, screaming her name. Diary, I swear I've never been so enraged or so determined in my life: no matter what, I would force Capucine to confess to whatever nonsense she'd invented to come between me and Sam!

"Where are you, Capucine?! I want to know what you said to Sam! Come on, show yourself, you big, fat, selfish liar!"
"Whoa! Relax . . ."

When I realized it was, in fact, Capucine's voice I was hearing floating up from the basement, I flew down the stairs two at a time. When I saw her standing there at the bottom, hands on her hips in the doorway to Dimitri's office, it took everything in me to stay calm.

"What did you say to Sam? Go on, spit it out!"
"What? I just told him the truth, Franny . . . About what you told me, in the bathroom at the party the other day. You don't remember?"
"Are you completely insane? WHAT are you talking about?!"
"Sam is my friend, and I think he has the right to know you have a boyfriend back home in Quebec. What did you say his name was again? Henry? Is that it?"

SILENCE.

I didn't know
where to begin

to explain everything to Sam—or even to Leif and Francine, who were obviously wondering what was going on. I was speechless, and Capucine was clearly loving every minute of it, staring at me with a mixture of satisfaction and condescending pity in her eyes.

"You know NOTHING about my life, Capucine! It's over with that guy Henry, okay?! Sam, you need to believe me. Here, look at my phone. You can read all my messages if you want. I texted him earlier to tell him . . . well, about us."

As I was pulling my phone out of my pocket, it suddenly dawned on me that I'd just admitted to Sam that I'd been lying to him all along.

"It's not what you think, Sam. I mean, I can explain everything."

I stopped talking then, when I realized every word that came out of my mouth . . .

only made me look more guilty to Sam
and more pathetic to Capucine.

I took a deep breath and glared at her. Just as I was thinking I might jump her (and tear off her cheap leatherette miniskirt), Dimitri broke the silence.

"WHAT are you doing in my office?"
"Dad, I tried to tell them. I didn't go in, don't worry."

GET OUUUUUT!

My father was standing right next to Dimitri. As you know, Diary, he's a LOUSY disciplinarian. So, when he tried his best to be strict too, it came out sounding more like this . . .

"That's right, everyone, um, upstairs."

But Dimitri was much more upset than we'd initially thought—abnormally upset, even.

"Get out of my house!"
". . ."

"Leave, immediately. And don't ever come back."
". . ."

"Any of you! And, Sam, go to your room."
"Yes, Dad."

I glanced at my father, completely baffled: I know Sam's dad works on super-mega-confidential projects, but to kick us out of his house . . . really? I mean, it's not like Capucine works for the FBI!

So, that's how we came to leave Sam's house and end up standing around my father's car. Incidentally, my dad looked even more upset than we did about what had just happened.

Dad: All right, let me drive you all home.
Franny: No way, Dad. Capucine is not getting in our car.
Capucine: Whatever. Like I would, anyway.
Leif: I'll walk Capucine home. You guys go ahead.
Dad: Right. Francine, are you going with them, then?
Francine: No.
Franny: You can sleep over at our house if you want.
Dad: Um, yes, of course, you're welcome to stay, Francine.

And that's how Francine ended up here, for a sleepover, after the weirdest and most pathetic pizza party on the planet.

// P.S. //

When we got home, Francine
and I made two huge mugs of hot cocoa
to cheer ourselves up. That's when
I decided to tell her everything about
Henry and the drama of the past few months.
Through a mouthful of marshmallows,
Francine proceeded to tell me my life
was way too complicated.
Then she convinced me I absolutely had
to call Sam.

"Like, now-now?"
"Yes, right now!"
"Haven't you ever heard the expression 'sleep on it,' Francine?"
"Franny, not everything in life can be summed up with a silly expression, okay? You want to be with Sam, right?"

"Well, I . . ."
"Are you happy with him, yes or no?"
"Yes."
"Then call him."

I still waited until Francine was sound asleep before working up the nerve to call Sam. And I have to admit I was shocked, Diary, because he actually picked up. Unlike Henry, who had ignored me for so long! My brain was foggy from exhaustion, but I still managed to explain everything. I mean:

THE REAL TRUTH.

And I know Sam believed me, or at least . . . he forgave me.

But he made me promise not to hide anything else from him, which I did—cross my heart, hope to die, stick a needle in my eye. As we hung up, I was left wondering why I couldn't do the same for Leona.

I mean,
why am I so incapable of
forgiveness?

F. x

Tuesday, April 18
9:20 p.m.

Emotional force field

"Dad, can I tell you something?"
"Yes, sweetheart."

When I walked into the kitchen tonight to talk to my father, I found him with his head buried in his giant encyclopedia. He's been reading nonstop for two days. I think it's his way of avoiding having to deal with his feelings.

Books and work are a little like his
emotional force field,
I think.

"I ran into old Manaka earlier . . ."
"Franny, really! You need to stop calling her that!"
"I know, sorry. I mean, I ran into Yoko's mother."
"Yeah, she told me you're helping her with her garden. Are you?"
"Yeah, a little. I keep messing up, but it's a good distraction for her, I think. And for me too."
"I'm happy to hear that."
"I have some news about the bonsai, Dad. It's all better."
"Oh . . . that's great."
"Yeah, don't sound so excited."
" . . ."
"Dad, you seem, I don't know . . . a little off these past few days."
"No, no, don't worry about it."
"It's because of the other night at Dimitri's, isn't it?"

Yeah, after seeing her bent over in her garden every day, I decided I couldn't let her keep doing all that work alone. Anyway, they say gardening is therapeutic. I figure it can't hurt, right? ⏎

WHEN MY FATHER TAKES OFF HIS GLASSES *It's a sign* HE'S LISTENING TO ME 110%

"Sam's dad has a really bad temper. Seriously! There was no need to freak out like that."

"Yeah, you're right, he is a little . . . uptight."

"I'm glad you're not like him."

"Ooh, a compliment! That's rare. Are you feeling okay, Franny?"

"Yeah, yeah . . ."

"Is it because you spoke to Leona?"

"No, not at all. Why?"

"Because you said you were on the phone with her on Saturday, just before we went over to Sam's."

"Oh. No, I . . ."

"I think it's a good thing you've decided to forgive her."

"Um . . ."

"You know, your mom and Leona's mom once had a huge fight too?"

"No! I didn't know that."

My father dropped his sad expression and launched into a story about how, long before I was born, Sylvie and my mother got into an argument. Like, a massive blowout.

I admit, I almost didn't believe it at first, but, apparently, my mother and Sylvie were both in love with—get this, Diary—him. That's right, my father! Apparently, they didn't speak to each other for a whole year! And for what? Because my mom agreed to go to prom with my dad, and Sylvie took it badly.

"So, how did they make up?"
"I told your mother I would break up with her if she didn't make the first move."
"No way. I don't believe you! You loved Mom too much."
"You're right. But your mother and Sylvie were so miserable. And Sylvie was even dating a new guy! I wasn't about to let them ruin the greatest friendship in history over a matter of pride!"
"And . . . that's it? I mean, they became friends again, just like that?!"
"In two minutes flat."
"Yeah . . ."

I KNOW what you're thinking, Diary. But things between Leona and me are 3,250 times more complicated than that. Ugh, I just had a thought . . .

> What if my emotional force field is my pride?

Anyway, force field or not, I need time. Because if—and that's a big *if*—I decide to forgive Leona, I want to be absolutely sure I'm ready when the time comes.

F. x

Japanese runaway

I PROMISE, it wasn't me who ran away. But that doesn't mean I'm not (at least partially) responsible for what happened today. And let's just say, rivalry or no rivalry, I would have never, ever forgiven myself if something bad had happened.

To Capucine, I mean.
She's the one who ran away today.

For starters, since Monday morning, I'd managed to keep my solemn vow never to speak to her again. And the situation at school had quickly gone viral: over the next few days, Capucine found herself more alone than ever as, one by one, all the other students (who'd started to hear rumors about what had happened on Saturday night) stopped talking to her.

It goes without saying that Ms. Clara eventually noticed the growing chill between her daughter and the rest of the universe. Which is why she decided to rip off the Band-Aid, right in the middle of biology class.

"Things have been tense in here all week! What's going on? Out with it."

— OBVIOUSLY, NO ONE ANSWERED HER. —

"Franny, Capucine, do either of you have any idea what's changed since Monday?"

"Um . . . no, Miss."

"Nope."

"Well, come to think of it, maybe I do. I think, well, it might be best . . . for everyone . . . if Capucine left our team. Our social science team. We just can't work with her anymore."

"Well, then . . . I imagine there's a good reason for this?"

"The reason is, well, Capucine is just mean. She's a liar, and no one can stand her! Not even the guy she has the hots for! So, that's, um , . . the reason."

I went a little too far,
dragging Sam into it,
and I knew it.

I also knew I should have consulted the others before kicking Capucine off the team, but just as I was about to apologize or walk things back or something, Francine stood up.

"I agree. I think it would be best if she left too. Sam, what do you think?"

I looked at Capucine out of the corner of my eye: she was acting like she couldn't care less, sitting at her desk with her arms crossed, but it was obvious she was waiting for Sam's answer, like some kind of verdict. After a long silence, Sam—without moving a muscle or even raising his eyes—finally spoke.

"I agree too. I think it would be best if Capucine found another team."

At the sound of the bell, Capucine stood up and grabbed her bag. She walked over to Leif and whispered something in his ear, then stormed out of the classroom before Ms. Clara could stop her.

Ms. Clara yelled after her: "Capucine! Get back here this instant! You four, you can bet we'll be talking about this!"

Ten minutes later, as I was sitting in front of a huge bowl of rice hidden under an unidentifiable pink substance, I started to feel really guilty, Diary. I mean, I had every right to want Capucine off our team, but maybe I hadn't needed to humiliate her the way I did . . .

. . . in front of the entire class?

I could tell Sam and Leif felt bad too, because they were just sitting there, staring wordlessly at their Jell-O, appetites gone. Just as I was starting to wonder where Francine was, we saw her stumble into the cafeteria.

"Cap . . . Capu . . ."
"Yeah, yeah, Capucine. Relax, Francine. What's going on?"
"She's gone! And she left this in our locker!"

Francine held out a note, written in Capucine's handwriting.

Now you can stop being ashamed of being MY SISTER.

C.

"Seriously, calm down. She probably just needed some air."
"You don't understand, Sam! She left without her medication! Her coat and boots are gone, but she left her bag behind."

When he heard that, Sam stopped talking
(even breathing, I think).

"Maybe she took her pills before leaving?"
"No, impossible. She needs to take them every day at exactly one o'clock."
"What's all this business about pills? Is Capucine sick?"

Francine and Sam (in unison): She takes ANTIEPILEPTICS!

"*Mon dieu!* Okay, okay, I didn't know . . ."
"If she doesn't take them, she'll have a seizure. Crap . . . If that happens while she's all alone, in the middle of the city, and no one knows what's wrong with her . . ."
"Calm down, we'll figure it out."
"It's 12:40, *ce n'est pas bon.*"
"No, not good at all."
"I'm going to tell your mother."
"No! My mother would never forgive me if something happened to her! It's my fault she's gone. It's all my fault . . ."

Francine started sobbing, and that's when Leif turned super serious. I almost didn't recognize him.

"I need to tell you guys something."
"What? What?!!!"
"Just before Capucine left class, she handed me . . . her phone."
"What? Why?"
"*Je ne sais pas.* Maybe she was trying to tell me something."

349

Leif took Capucine's phone out of his bag. We knew we didn't have a second to lose, so when we realized it was locked, we started freaking out. But thankfully, Sam knew the code.

"I'm *très, très* sorry. I have no idea why she gave it to me."
"Hand it over."

In a frenzy, Francine opened all the apps on Capucine's phone. When she started scrolling through a series of photos, we realized she'd found something important. She stared at them, one after another. Sam grabbed the phone, desperate to know what was going on.

"What is all this? It doesn't mean anything!"
"I'm not sure, but I think they're pictures of your dad's research, Franny. Look, Sam, my sister took these pictures in your father's office. If you zoom in, right here, you can see."

"So, that's what she was doing . . . in your father's office? She was taking pictures?"
"But . . . why?"
"I have no idea. How should I know?!"
"Okay, there's no point standing here staring at these pictures! We need to figure out where she went."

When I saw Sam, Francine, and Leif panicking at the thought of something happening to Capucine, I realized she was a thousand times less alone than she probably thought.

Instead of dwelling on the (ultra-sketchy) pictures of the research papers or even listening to Francine's list of the top-ten worst things that could happen, I got down to thinking.

"So, um, when I feel sad, I like to hide in closets."
"*Quoi?!* What are you talking about, Franny?"
"Okay, guys, where do people go when they're sad?"
"Franny, this really isn't the time for riddles!"
"I know. I'm honestly trying to think. Where do they go?"
"Well, I don't know. They go somewhere that makes them feel safe, I guess."
"Sam, didn't you say Capucine always used to take you to the same place, when you guys were dating?"
"The fox park."
"What?"
"Yeah, I know, it's weird, but there's a fox park in Kyoto, and she goes there all the time. If we leave now, we can be there in twenty minutes."
"Okay, what are we waiting for? Let's go!"

PART 2

THE LINGERING TASTE OF DISASTER WITH JUST A HINT OF TAME FOX

We only had two bikes, so Sam and Leif doubled with me and Francine. We kept screaming at them to pedal faster, and Sam kept repeating "We're almost there, we're almost there," but it did nothing to calm Francine, who stared at the time on her phone the entire way there.

"We're here."
"*Merde*, it's closed."

Sam and Leif came to a stop in front of a massive padlocked gate. The sign on it read:

My translation.
Obviously, it was written in Japanese.

 # Kyomizu dera / Fox sanctuary

Clouds had rolled in overhead, turning the mood even more dramatic—like we really needed more drama. Francine tugged frantically on the padlock, to no avail.

I yanked off my mittens and started scaling the tall fence. Sam called out to me, but it was one of those moments where thinking twice wasn't an option.

"Franny, you're going to hurt yourself. We'll find another way in!"
"Don't worry, Sam, I've done this before!"

Mid-climb, I was suddenly struck with an intense feeling of déjà vu. As I struggled to make it over the top of the fence, bracing myself with my legs and gripping onto the metal bars for dear life, images of Henry and Leona began flashing through my mind. And I started thinking about that night, in the cemetery, when my friends had risked everything to follow me to Old Man Birgman's place.

Henry . . .
standing there waiting for me
on the other side of the garden fence
even though he was terrified.

Leo . . .
screaming her
head off.

because she feared the worst.

And I couldn't help thinking,
ultimately, that must be what

real friends do, in life:
risk everything.

I froze at the top of the fence, paralyzed by that thought. Sam was screaming at me, but I didn't hear him.

"Franny! What are you doing? Get down from there. You're going to get hurt!"

How could I have
forgotten my two best friends
so quickly and . . . so easily?

But I snapped out of it pretty quickly when my body suddenly plunged ten feet through the air. I also realized I'd probably just been seriously hurt trying to play the superhero.

"Ouch! Crap, my ankle!"
"I told you, Franny! Stay there. We'll go get help! We don't even know if Capucine is here. What were you thinking? How are you going to get back over?"

I braced myself and stood up, thinking if there was even a one-in-a-million chance Capucine was here, I'd find her.

"Francine, throw me your sister's bag! Her medication! Throw it over!"

Francine hurled the bag over the fence, and I caught it in midair. Just before entering the sanctuary, I turned to look back at my friends, for a shot of courage. When I saw they were already rushing away—to get help, no doubt—I was overcome by a weird dizzy feeling. But I shoved down the fear in my heart.

And let me tell you, Diary, with its endlessly tall, bare trees, there was nothing comforting about the place. After ten minutes of walking in circles around the sanctuary (which is an awful lot like a maze, come to think of it), I started thinking I must've gotten it all wrong, yet again. Then I started talking to myself, which was a very bad sign indeed:

"What were they thinking, calling this place a fox sanctuary? Seriously! There's nothing but pathetic-looking trees here! Where are you, you stupid Japanese foxes?"

No sooner had I said that than I saw a long orange streak disappear behind a stone wall not fifty feet away. I tiptoed forward, failing to notice that the gloomy forest had given way to a big, open clearing: the fox sanctuary, I guess.

And that's when
I saw her.

CURLED UP IN A BALL ON A ROCK, HOOD PULLED OVER HER HEAD, CAPUCINE WAS THERE.

Like a fox with razor-sharp instincts, she'd sensed my presence long before I spotted her:

"What do you want?"

I stood there, unmoving, for a good minute, not sure how to approach her, but mostly not sure what to say.

Maybe humans are a little like foxes sometimes?

"I came to say, well, that I'm sorry."
"Go away, Franny. I don't need your pity."
"It's not pity. I know how you feel, believe me."

"You don't know anything, Franny.
Okay? Nothing."

When I realized Capucine wasn't going to listen to a word I had to say,
it reminded me of the time Leona had provoked me, to force me out
of my three-day cryfest over the whole Henry thing. It had taken her
lighting a fire under my butt to get me out of bed. So, I thought to
myself: *if there's one thing you know how to do, Franny Cloutier,
it's stir up trouble! So, what are you waiting for?*

"You think you're the only person who's afraid? Who thinks your life
sucks? Who feels like things aren't going EXACTLY as planned? Well,
I have news for you, Capucine. We're all in the same boat, okay? And
starting now, you have two choices. Either you can stay here all alone
with the foxes, feeling sorry for yourself for the rest of your life, or you
can get up, watch the sun rise and set every day . . . and try to find a
little happiness in between!"

Capucine stared straight ahead, toward the horizon. At first, she was
so stone faced that I thought my tactic had failed. But then she started
to shake. The only problem was, I didn't realize what was happening
because I was so annoyed by her indifference.

"I . . . I forgot to take . . ."
"Ugh, forget it, Capucine. You're a lost cause, anyway."
"No, Franny! . . . I need you."
"Oh, really? NOW you need me!"
"I forgot my bag at school. And, well, there's something in it I really
need . . . Right now."
"Oh."
"Franny, this is serious, I swear."
"I know. I mean, don't worry, I have them, your pills!"

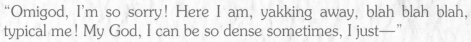

"Omigod, I'm so sorry! Here I am, yakking away, blah blah blah, typical me! My God, I can be so dense sometimes, I just—"
"Franny, stop talking. I don't know why you have my bag, but just give me my medication."
"Um, yeah. Here."

I'll spare you the details, Diary, but the good news is, despite my verbal diarrhea, Capucine managed to take her pills in time, or just about. So, medical disaster averted (just barely).

Once that was taken care of, we just sat there, staring straight ahead, wordlessly, for a really long time.

Capucine finally
broke the silence.

"Franny, you're bleeding."
"I know, I fell climbing the fence."
"Which fence?"
"You know, the one with the lock, at the entrance to the park?"
"Oh."
"What do you mean, 'oh'?"
"Well, next time . . . you can just go through the bushes, next to the front gate."
"Seriously?"
"Yup. Seriously."

I looked at Capucine, and just like that, for no reason at all, we burst out laughing. I couldn't stop, even though my ankle was killing me. I wasn't really laughing about the fence, Diary, but more because I was relieved that I'd maybe (and that's a big maybe) managed to make peace with Capucine. And I could tell she was happy about it too.

At that exact moment, Leif, Francine, and Sam ran into the sanctuary. They were with the security guard, who, by the way, didn't look too pleased that a gang of teenagers had found their way into his park. When they saw us laughing, they stopped dead in their tracks—I admit, it was pretty surreal.

— And it was followed by —
big reconciliations,
big hugs,
big emotions.

We eventually left the sanctuary, under the bewildered gaze of the security guard, who didn't understand A SINGLE WORD of our story about Capucine's pills and our argument and her running away—which she didn't really do, come to think of it.

(I'm really starting to think something's going on between those two . . .)

On the way back, Capucine sat next to Leif.
As we were getting off the bus, she called out to us:

"Hey, do you guys think you could . . . promise me something?"
" . . . "
"Think you could keep my epilepsy a secret? I really don't want the whole school knowing."

Francine stepped off the bus, then turned to face Capucine.

"All right. But on two conditions."
"What?"
"First, you make an effort to be nice. Like, for real, Capucine."
"And second?"
"You EXPLAIN what you were doing in Sam's father's office and why you took all those pictures."
"Ah."

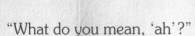

"What do you mean, 'ah'?"

"Well, I . . ."

"Capucine."

"I think we need to sit down for this."

"Sit down?"

"Yeah. Let's find somewhere quiet, and I promise I'll tell you everything."

"Fine, after you."

I got a really bad feeling when she said that, Diary. I mean, it's never a good sign when someone asks you to sit down before telling you something, right?

Everybody
knows that.
F.

P.S.
On the bus ride home, I did the most impulsive thing ever: I texted Leona. I SWEAR! I don't really know how to explain it, but it's like I suddenly realized that I'd betrayed Leona too. That's right. The time I stole the postcard she sent her mom from New York; I was so selfish, thinking only of myself. Anyway, I just did it, because I knew if I put it off until later, I might chicken out.

361

So, here's what I wrote, basically:

Franny - 2:31 p.m.

Hey, Leona.
I can't talk right now.
A girl from my school ran away, and we just found her in a fox park, just in time to give her her medication. It sounds complicated, I know. But give me a little more time, and then I'd really love to talk. Later!

P.P.S.
I knew full well my father
would grill me again
at dinner tonight.
I had eight missed calls
from him. He'd obviously just spent
his entire Friday afternoon
waiting for us at his lab.

PART 3

It took FOREVER for Capucine to work up the courage to explain what she was doing in Sam's father's office last Saturday. But the second she started talking, Diary, it all became clear. Clear that my life in Japan might be over much sooner than I'd thought. Clear, also, that my father's dream might be hanging on only by a thread: namely, me.

I know. I need to start at the beginning.
So, here goes.

The five of us ended up sitting on the floor, surrounded by a mountain of cushions, five bottles of soda, and about twenty cats. Yes, cats. Leif had suggested we talk at a cat café. I swear, it's a real thing, and it's super popular in Japan. Weird, I know.

— But THAT'S not what I need to tell you. —

Capucine cracked all ten fingers, one by one, before she started talking. We were clearly just as nervous as she was: we knew if she'd asked us all to sit down, she obviously had something big to tell us.

Incidentally, if we hadn't just made up an hour earlier, I would have sworn she was doing it on purpose—dragging out the suspense and hogging all the attention. Sam was the first one to lose his patience.

"You wanted us to sit down? We're sitting down. You even have an audience of two hundred cats. What's going on, Capucine?"
"I'm not sure of anything, Sam."
"That's too bad, but just spill it! What were you doing in my father's office?"

"I'm not sure what made me go in, but I know what I found. And the truth is . . . it's only going to end up hurting you all. Especially you, Sam."

"If this is a joke, Capucine, it's not very funny."

Leif took Capucine's phone out of his sweater pocket. He put it down in front of him, a serious look on his face.

"It's not a joke. I read everything, on the bus. Capucine took pictures of a paper that talks about the foundation Sam's dad plans to start."

"I know all about that, Leif. And by the way, it's my father's foundation too. To eliminate aging, or something like that. He's already told me all about it."

"Well, that's the problem, Franny."

"What are you talking about?"

"Your father's name doesn't appear anywhere. Like, nowhere."

"*Bien*, except for one place, you mean."

"Yeah."

Leif and Capucine were way too in sync, and they were obviously the only ones who knew what was going on.

"We're pretty sure Sam's father never had any intention of making your dad a partner in the foundation."

"Once your dad is finished with his research, Sam's father plans to fire him, Franny."

"What ON EARTH are you talking about?! That's impossible. It's his idea, his research, his theory. It's his entire life! I know you don't like Sam's father, but this is all a bit much, really."

"Here. Read it for yourself, Franny."

367

Just as I was starting to calm down, to convince myself that Capucine had imagined it all and that her stupid pile of pictures meant nothing, my eyes landed on her phone screen. It was an entire paragraph about my father, and I must have read it at least ten times, searching desperately for a loophole, an error, a mistake that would prove it was all just a misunderstanding.

But Leif and Capucine were right.
And I was
forced
to admit it.

— Here's what it said, essentially. —

Note that Hubert Cloutier,
initially involved in the project
as a paid anonymous researcher (details in appendix),
shall be terminated immediately upon opening of the
research center.
A team of experienced scientists shall be put in place
to take over operations,
and the work done by Mr. Cloutier shall be
subjected to rigorous verifications.

I sat there staring at Capucine's phone for a good minute, wondering what was worse.

Having to admit
that this entire story might actually be
true?

Or . . .

The terrible knowledge that these pictures had

THE POWER TO DESTROY MY FATHER'S DREAM.

When I finally snapped out of it, I felt Sam lay his hand on top of mine. From the way he touched me, I knew he'd read it, and that he knew what was going on. I could also tell he was ashamed:

His father had been exposed for what he really was, and there was nothing Sam could do about it.

I don't know why, Diary, but at that exact moment, I just didn't have the strength to look Sam in the eye. Even though I knew all he wanted was some kind of sign, some reassurance that this wouldn't drive us apart, that I didn't blame him for being blindsided, and that I knew he'd had nothing to do with any of this.

But I couldn't bring myself to say any of that. So, I looked away and let my silence speak for itself.

I've been naïve in the past, but this time, I need to protect my family. So, until I'm completely sure Sam had NO idea about his father's treacherous plans . . .

369

— THERE'S NO WAY —
I can trust him.

That's what my silence meant. And Sam got the message . . . because he stood up to leave. But just before the door closed behind him, he called out to me one last time.

"I'm not like him, Franny."

" . . . "

"I'm going to talk to my father."

After Sam left, we all decided to go home. Francine has texted me seven times since then, but I really need to be alone, Diary, so I didn't reply.

I've been home for an hour, and thankfully my father isn't back yet. Good thing because I seriously don't think I have the guts to tell him everything I know. Not tonight, anyway. But honestly, I also don't know how I'll be able to keep it from him much longer.

This is what's called "being at an impasse."

The last time I had a terrible feeling like this

was when I found out the truth about my mother.

AND I WAS RIGHT X 1,000

MOM IN 1998

Mom, if you're listening,
Dad and I really need you right now. Like, a lot.
I really wish I knew what you'd do right now, if you were me.

Later,
F. x

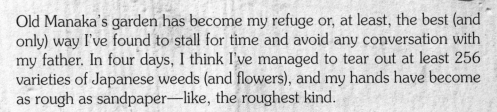

Stalling for time

Old Manaka's garden has become my refuge or, at least, the best (and only) way I've found to stall for time and avoid any conversation with my father. In four days, I think I've managed to tear out at least 256 varieties of Japanese weeds (and flowers), and my hands have become as rough as sandpaper—like, the roughest kind.

When old Manaka sat down next to me in the yard tonight, I realized that—unlike my father—she hadn't been fooled for even one second by my sudden passion for plants.

"Oh! I see you've managed to tear up every last living thing in my garden, Fubuki."

I raised my head, not quite sure what to say.

"I know. I'm sorry. I'll buy you new flowers, Manaka."
"Your father is worried about you, Franny. Apparently you're no longer speaking to any of your friends. In Quebec or here . . ."
"My father said that?"
" . . . "
"Well, if you ask me, he should be a million times more worried about himself."

The second those words came out of my mouth, I knew I'd just opened a Pandora's box. But Manaka didn't react, and oddly enough, that gave me the confidence I needed. What I mean is, it made me feel like I could open up to her. And that's how, both hands buried up to my

wrists in dirt, and without the least bit of forethought, I ended up telling her the deep, dark secret I'd been carrying around for four days.

She listened right to the very end. Then, in typical Manaka fashion, she said a great deal (in not so many words).

"I think you know exactly what you need to do, Fubuki."
"No! I swear, I don't, Manaka!"
"Are you . . . certain?"
". . ."
"Because I believe we very often know which road to take, but it's the fear of what might happen next . . . that paralyzes us."

I love old Manaka, but her knack for always being right really gets on my nerves.

It's decided.

One day, I'll be old and wise and wrinkly, and I'll preach at everyone too. But, until then, I think I've done enough gardening. I have NO CLUE how I'll manage, but I do know one thing: my father has a right to know the truth.

Later,
Franny

Priorities, priorities

Leona

> It's taken everything I have not to text you,
> but it's been A WEEK since you said you
> wanted to talk!
> And no news since your weird fox story.
> You know, if you've changed your mind, you can just
> tell me.

Leona's text was the first thing I saw when I opened my eyes this morning. Needless to say, I wrote back right away. I definitely hadn't changed my mind, but the drama of the past few days had monopolized all my attention.

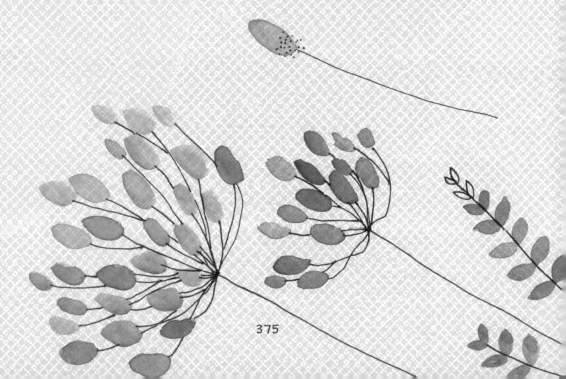

TEXT THREAD

April 26, 7:33 a.m. Kyoto time
April 25, 6:33 p.m. Quebec time

Franny

I haven't forgotten about you, I promise.
And I owe you an apology.
For real.

Leona

Come on, I'M the one who should apologize.

Franny

I never gave you the chance to explain yourself.
I just tried to cut you out of my life.
After everything you did for me.

Leona

Maybe,
but I betrayed you.

Franny

Maybe,
but I never stopped to think how you must've felt,
not even for half a second.

Leona

Do you really mean that?

Franny

I don't want us to fight anymore.
Especially over a guy.

Leona

I know. Me either.
So, what now?

Franny

I don't know.
Clean slate?

Leona

Absolutely.

Leona

:)

Franny

But do you think you could do me
a tiny little favor?

Leona

You don't waste any time, do you?! ;)

Leona

Kidding! What is it?

Franny

Ha ha, nope.
Could you tell Henry
that I'd really like to talk to him,
but I need some time.
I have some really major things to figure out here,
but there's something I need to tell him.
I just can't right now.

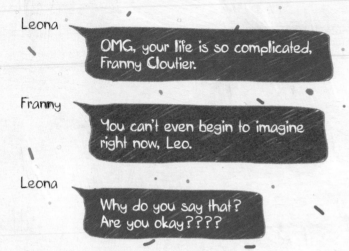

Leona: OMG, your life is so complicated, Franny Cloutier.

Franny: You can't even begin to imagine right now, Leo.

Leona: Why do you say that? Are you okay????

Honestly, I was dying to tell Leona everything, but I knew I had to get my priorities straight: I didn't really see how Leona could help me from St. Lorette.

Franny: It's a really long story, but I'll fill you in soon.

Leona: Okay . . . but when?

Franny: Really soon, pinkie promise. Just give me a few days. Xx

Leona: Okay xxx

Hard to say whether it was because I'd made up with Leona or because of Manaka's advice, but when I got to school this morning, things seemed, well, less complicated. One thing was sure, I knew what I had to do, and I knew I couldn't do it without my friends.

So, school or no school,
I had to find a way
to talk to Leif, Francine, Capucine,

and obviously ... Sam.

The only problem is, I was pretty sure they weren't impressed with the fact I've been ignoring them these past few days. So, when I got to class, I turned on **ALL MY CHARM** to convince them to give me another chance. I signaled them over to my desk, a pleading look in my eyes. They took their sweet time, but eventually the five of us were gathered together. ← By the way, I sprained my ankle at the fox park. So, I'm in pain AND my right foot is all wrapped up in a bandage BUT I'm allowed to wear my Converse at school.

"I know what you're going to say, but we have 3 minutes and 24 seconds until the bell rings, so can you at least give me that much time to explain?"

Francine sighed and crossed her arms over her chest. Bad sign, I thought.

"I know this is all really hard for you, but you can't just ignore us like you've done since Friday and hope we'll still be there for you!"
"I agree. *Pas cool.*"
"I know. I just . . ."
"I'm willing to hear you out." ← Clearly, Capucine is keeping promise no. 1 (be nice)
"Sam, what about you?"

"I don't know, have you decided to trust me now?"
"Yes, I think so. I mean, yes, I trust you."

Obviously, my hesitation was a bit much. I realized then that something between me and Sam had been broken last Friday, only I wasn't quite sure what. But I banished that thought from my mind: I was a thousand times more worried about having to break the news to my father all alone.

I was relieved to hear that Sam had decided not to say anything to his father, and that apart from us (oh, and old Manaka), no one knew my father was about to be fired from his own research project. So, by the time the bell rang, we had the start of a plan.

At exactly 1 p.m. tomorrow, we'd go to my father's lab, as planned.
That's when we would tell him EVERYTHING.
And, um, we'd figure out the rest.
No choice.

To be continued . . .

(I have to go, I'm in gym class.
I'm pretending to have period cramps because I hate soccer. My cardio sucks.)

Franny xo

Thursday, April 27
10:53 p.m.

(Drastic)
change of plans

When I got home from school, my father was sitting by himself at the kitchen table. He wasn't reading. He wasn't cooking. He wasn't even moving. He was completely neutral. Weird, I thought.

"What are you doing, Dad? Why aren't you at work?"
"I was waiting for you."

OBJECTIVE:
avoid all serious conversation with him.

"Oh, that's too bad . . . because I have a ton of homework to do."
"Franny, come sit down."

Have I mentioned my father has an impeccable sense of timing? I mean, I was already planning to tell him everything in less than 24 hours, but then he decides we need to have some major FATHER-DAUGHTER conversation tonight! Meaning?

I was caught completely off guard, which led to . . .

this.

"What's going on? Have I done something wrong?"

"Of course not, Franny. Stink bug, I wanted to talk to you because I've been doing a lot of thinking lately."

". . . Okay."

"And I wanted to tell you, I know I haven't been there for you enough these past few months. And that all that's going to change."

Come to think of it, I think I prefer "neutral" dad

to "change" dad.

"I'm going to tell Dimitri things can't go on like this. If he wants to work with me, we need to slow down. Do things MY way. Our way, Franny!"

My father stood up, overcome by his sudden surge of determination.

"And I'll tell him he can take it or leave it! I won't stand for him treating me like an employee!"

I didn't need to stand up or even look my father in the eye for him to grasp the seriousness of my warning. Just my tone of voice was enough.

"Dad, don't do that."

". . ."

"He'd be only too happy to see you go."

That stopped my father dead in his tracks. He stared at me, question marks flashing in his eyes. And that's how—without an ounce of preparation or rehearsal—I was forced to tell him everything.

Obviously, in the moment he refused to believe me.

"Sweetheart, I know you don't like it here. And I promise things will get better. But making up stories like that about Dimitri isn't how you'll—"
"Dad, it has nothing to do with Japan, I swear. If I'd wanted us to leave, believe me, I would have found a much easier way a long time ago. You know me better than that!"
"You're right, I do know you, Franny."

From the massively skeptical look still plastered across my father's face, I knew he'd NEVER BELIEVE A WORD of what I'd just said without seeing some evidence. So, I texted Capucine and asked her to send me all the photos she'd taken in Sam's father's office. Twelve minutes later, my father was forced to admit I was telling the truth.

The weirdest thing is, Diary, I'm still not absolutely convinced I did the right thing. I mean, our entire world collapsed tonight because I spilled the beans. And now I have no control over anything! Every single crease and line on my father's face is screaming complete and utter . . . devastation.

That's right.

MY FATHER

is simply

DESTROYED.

MAY

A television and a dream shattered to pieces

"Franny, I need to be alone, please."
"Yeah, of course."
" . . . "
"I'll be in my room, Dad."

I KNOW.
Under the circumstances, eight days without an entry
could be considered an eternity.

— But read on, and you'll understand. —

REASON n°1

As you can see, I don't have many blank pages left, and I knew—given everything that's happened lately—that I'd really, really need you, Diary.

REASON n°2

I've been super busy for the past week. Let's just say, over the past seven days, Sam, my father, my sprained ankle (which is really killing me), and life in general have sucked up ABSOLUTELY all my energy. Why, you ask?

For starters, once my father got over the initial shock, his hurt and embarrassment at being betrayed by Sam's father gave way to an unimaginable fury. I swear, I never knew my father was capable of that much rage.

I wasn't there last Saturday when he took it into his head to go over to Dimitri's house to confront him in person. But according to Sam, after they talked for a really long time, my father actually picked up the TV and threw it against the wall. So not like him! He's normally the peaceful-zen-chill type. But thankfully Yoko was there, and she convinced him to leave before he demolished the entire house (and his reputation).

WoW

The good news is, even though Sam's just as upset as I am about what happened, I don't think it's come between us as much as I thought. I mean, we're obviously not dating anymore (judging from the six feet of distance between us every time we talk), but at least we're not ignoring each other either.

That counts for something. Don't you think?

Honestly, I don't know what's going to happen between me and Sam. I'm not even sure we could work as a couple, given everything we know. But I really don't have time to think about it, because I have a much bigger problem to deal with:

We have exactly seven days before we need to hand in our social science project and give our report in front of the entire school, and we have NO IDEA what we're going to do!

But I do know one thing: Ms. Clara is going to kill us when she finds out we haven't spent a single afternoon at my father's lab during the past six weeks of so-called "research time."

I have to go, Diary. You won't believe it, but Sam just texted me a second ago to say he's at the door. My door! I swear, I'm not imagining it. This is what he just wrote me:

"Hey. I'm here ... outside your door."

Is he insane? It's 9:34 p.m. and (major detail) I'm in sweatpants. Anyway. I'll write again later ....

Bye, F.

(Same day)
11:01 p.m.

My (non) first time

Sam just left. And I think I did what I needed to do. Scratch that, I know I did what I needed to do. The more I think about it, the more I'm almost absolutely sure I just had my "non first time."

A "non first time"
is when it COULD have happened,
but it DIDN'T happen.

When I opened the door and saw that Sam was in fact there, and that
he'd gone to the trouble of bringing a big bouquet of yellow daisies, I
realized he'd come with the intention of making up with me.

"Let's go to my room. My dad can't know you're here."
"Why not? He doesn't want us to see each other anymore?"
"No, it's not that. It's almost ten o'clock, Sam. It's a weeknight, and . . .
well, I'm not really allowed to have guys in my bedroom."
"Oh. Okay . . ."

SAM FOLLOWED ME BACK TO MY ROOM

Yes
TO MY ROOM

I know, I was playing with fire. But I took precautions.

After closing the door behind me, I wedged a chair under the door handle. (By the way, I'm not convinced that chair thing works, but I've seen it a million times in action movies, so I thought it was worth a try!)

I put on music (Lady Gaga—not at all appropriate, but whatever), hoping it would muffle the sound of our voices; but obviously, my father's not deaf.

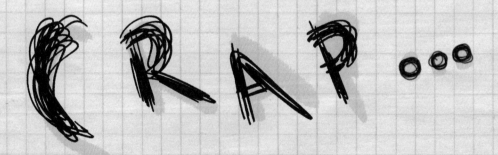

CRAP...

"Stink bug? Who are you talking to?"
"Um, I'm on the phone with Leona!"
"Are you in the kitchen?"
"I'm going to bed, Dad, good night!"
"Let me just come give you a kiss, sweetheart."
"No, I said I'M SLEEPING!"
"I hear music."
"It helps me sleep. Would you back off, geez!"
"Okay, okay . . ."

My God, my father
chooses the worst times
to be annoying.

I sat down on the end of my bed—totally not thinking Sam might take it as an invitation to join me. Which is how we ended up sitting next to each other, in a silence that was **NOT AT ALL** comfortable. I'm not sure what Sam was thinking might happen amid my six pillows and fluffy down comforter, but I was freaking out just imagining the possibilities.

I stayed frozen there, staring at him. Ridiculous, I know. I was holding the bouquet of daisies like a shield, stupidly hoping Sam would say something comforting or funny or even totally dumb.

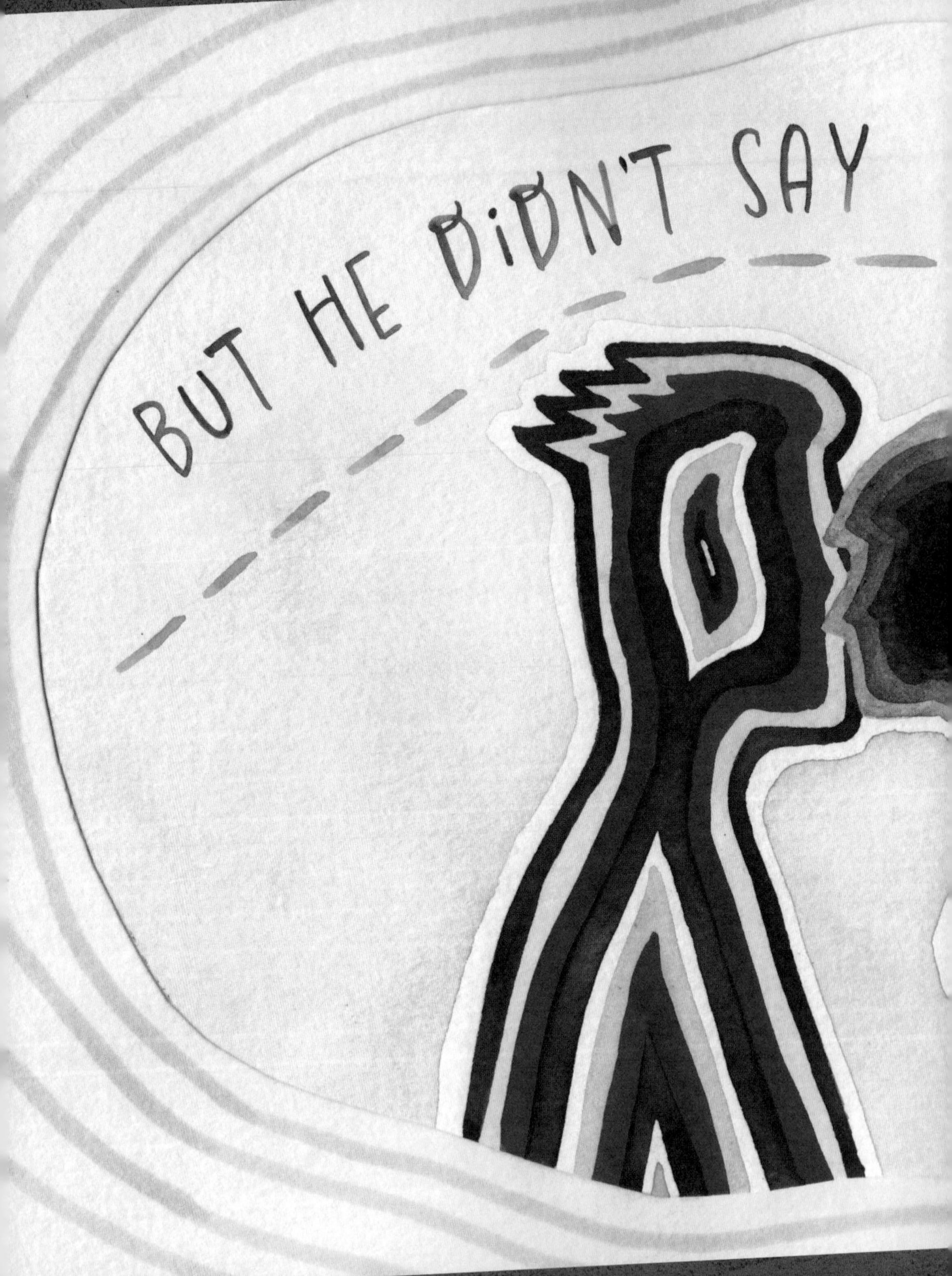
BUT HE DIDN'T SAY

A WORD

Instead,
he leaned in toward me
and kissed me.
At that point, my entire body collapsed
backward onto my bed,
and I was powerless to stop it.
Needless to say, the situation spiraled
COMPLETELY out of control when Sam's body
collapsed forward, and the
two of us ended up
horizontal.

Sam on top of me.
Me under Sam.
Totally awkward.

And to add to the stress, I couldn't stop thinking about my father and the international incident it would cause if he happened to walk into my room and witness what was going on, less than thirty feet away from him.

Just as I was thinking, *What if Sam tries to put his hand up my shirt?* I had a revelation, Diary. I realized that, no matter what Sam was hoping for, it just wasn't going to happen.

Let me explain. I know he wasn't expecting anything from me and that I'd probably imagined it all and he (most likely) had no specific intentions. But I had to face the facts: I'm not ready *for my first time*—or even for anything remotely resembling it.

Not tonight.
Not like this.
And (even though I like him a lot) not . . .

with him.

"Sam, stop."

He sat up. Like, instantly. He stared for a long while at my bedroom floor.

"It's because of that other guy. Henry . . . right?"

I could tell from Sam's voice that he wasn't mad or annoyed. More like sad. Which made me feel better. Like, it lifted a 500-million-pound weight off my shoulders. I sat up too, straightened out my hair, and gathered every spare ounce of courage to look him in the eyes.

I knew I owed him at
least that much.

"Yeah, I think so."

I hadn't given much thought to my answer, Diary, but I swear it was ultra sincere. What I mean is, even though I have NO IDEA when the "right time" might be, I think I'd want it to be with Henry.

It reminded me of what old Manaka said to me this week, about how we often already have the answers to our questions deep inside us. And I realized it must also mean that if we ignore our inner voice, we can end up convincing ourselves about a ton of crazy stuff, for a really long time.

So, I feel really bad saying this, but the truth is, I always knew that being with Sam would never be the same as . . . being with Henry.

NEVER

And the strangest thing about all this, Diary,
is that I can't really explain
why.

It's just something
I know.

"Sam."

"Don't say anything, Franny."

" . . . "

"I just hope this Henry knows how lucky he is."

Obviously, I didn't say anything.
And obviously, he left.

I wanted to call out to him: "**Please stay, Sam. You're my favorite person in Japan, I don't want to lose you,**" but I didn't. Out of shyness, out of respect, out of friendship, I suppose. I just sat on my bed, paralyzed, incapable of moving, until I heard the front door close.

Then I started picturing Sam, walking all alone through the streets of Kyoto. I also thought about Henry, going about his life on the other side of the world, never suspecting for even half a second that he'd just been the catalyst for a breakup in Japan. I also thought: no matter what happens, I'll know that I made the right decision. And that's all that matters.

Now I can only hope
Sam will still
want to be my friend.

And I can only hope
Henry will still
want me (period).

Later,
Franny

398

ST. LORETTE

Bras and zits
in the middle of the night

It's official.
I need to explain the concept of time zones
to Leona.

THERE'S A
13-HOUR
DIFFERENCE
BETWEEN JAPAN AND QUEBEC!!!

Not that hard to remember, right?!

In the meantime, Leo woke me up at four o'clock
in the morning to chat about her bra size, her
zits, and a letter that's going to take way too
long to get here.

TEXT THREAD

MAY 7, 4:08 a.m. Kyoto time
MAY 6, 3:08 p.m. Quebec time

Leona

I need to talk to you.

Leona

Franny, 911!!!

Franny

OMG, Leo, this better be important.
It's 4 a.m.

Leona

OMG, sorry!!!!!!!!
I totally SUCK with the time difference.
So sorry. Text me back when you're up.

Franny

Too late now.
It's okay, I haven't slept all weekend.

Leona

Why not??

Franny

Because of my ex, I think.

Leona

Your EX???
I didn't even know you had a boyfriend.

Franny

Yeah. I broke up with him, but it's okay.
It's complicated.

Franny

So, what's with the 911?!

Leona

I have a total pizza face, zits everywhere,
I'm FREAKING OUT.
So, I started taking the pill.

Leona

The birth control pill!!! Hello?!
I've gained AT LEAST 3 pounds.
And my boobs have, like, doubled in size. I'm a 34B now.

Franny

?

Leona

I'm talking about my BRA SIZE.

Franny

I KNOW. I'm not STUPID.
But seriously, you wake me up in the middle of the night
to talk about your bra size?!!

Leona

No.
I talked to Henry.

Franny

AND
?!?!?!?!??!?!!??!

Leona

All he said was that he sent you a letter.
And that you'd understand everything once you read it.

Franny

OMG, are you KIDDING ME?!
It'll take months
to get here.

Leona

He mailed it yesterday, so technically,
you should have it in about 7 days.
I checked.

Franny

Ugh, not cool.
But it's nice to have a nerdy friend.

Leona

Hey! I'm not a nerd!!

Franny

I know :) Mind if I go back to sleep now??
I'm tired!!

Leona

Of course not.
Night.

Franny

Night xxxx

P.S. //

My father is in the kitchen, making
pancakes with Yoko. I think that's a
good sign. I think it means he's
not completely and totally shattered.

So, even though it's definitely a good
thing he hasn't been back to his laboratory
since Thursday night, I'm still freaking out
because now I have no idea what's going
to happen to us.

I mean, if my father isn't
working on his research anymore,
I really don't see why we'd stay here in Japan.

I need to
clear things
up with him.
And fast.

Later,
F. xx

Wednesday, May 10
9:24 p.m.

Negotiating the truth:
NO WAY

Even though I admit Sam has a real knack for solving problems, that doesn't mean he should assume he's always right.

Let me explain.

 Leif, Francine, Capucine, Sam, and I all agreed on Monday that it was high time we told Ms. Clara we won't be able to present our social science project (in front of the entire school!!!) on Friday.

 Despite imagining every possible reaction from our teacher, we never dreamed Ms. Clara would react the way she did! Suffice it to say, when we broke the news to her at lunchtime on Tuesday, she didn't say A SINGLE WORD. She simply listened to us, then sat down at her desk with the most skeptical look I've ever seen in my entire life, Diary. It was plain to see Ms. Clara was wondering whether we were telling her

the whole truth,
and nothing but the truth.

 Out of desperation and figuring we had nothing to lose anyway—except for 30% of our social science grade—I decided to take matters into my own hands.

"Just because you don't like the truth, Ms. Clara, doesn't mean we're lying to you. And look! I have a sprained ankle! That's proof enough, right?"

"I'd never say something so serious about my own father if I wasn't absolutely convinced it's true, Ms. Clara."

Obviously, Sam couldn't have come up with a better argument to convince Ms. Clara, who suddenly seemed willing to consider the possibility we were telling the truth.

 Last, but not least:
I really don't know if Ms. Clara is going to give us an exemption on our social science project because of everything that's happened. All she said was she needs time to "figure everything out," but I do know one thing:

My new friendship with Sam has to be
—after old Manaka's bonsai—
the most fragile thing in this country.

After Ms. Clara left, the five of us just stood there, unmoving, in the middle of the classroom. Visibly, we were just as shaken up as our teacher, like telling her our story had only made things more real, more irrevocably real.

As we were about to head to the cafeteria for lunch, Sam asked me if we could talk. At first, I thought he wanted to talk about Friday night, but apparently the tattered remains of our relationship are the last thing on his mind right now.

"I spoke to my father."
"Well, he is your father."
"I wanted to tell you he's planning to offer your father money."
"What?"
"Like . . . a lot of money."
"Whatever! He's wrong if he thinks he can buy people off just because he's rich."
"Chill, Franny. My father's not a monster. He made a mistake, and, believe me, he knows it. At least he's trying to find a way to fix things."
"Fix things? Excuse me?"
"Anyway, it's none of our business. It's between them, and that's what my father's planning to do. I just wanted to let you know."

Sam left after that. Blew out like a big gust of wind, leaving me behind like a dirty old sock. It's weird, Diary, how some people think getting the last word means they've won. Not true, if you ask me. If Sam thinks everything in life can be negotiated, he's in for a BIG shock.

Too annoyed to keep writing.

Later,
Franny.

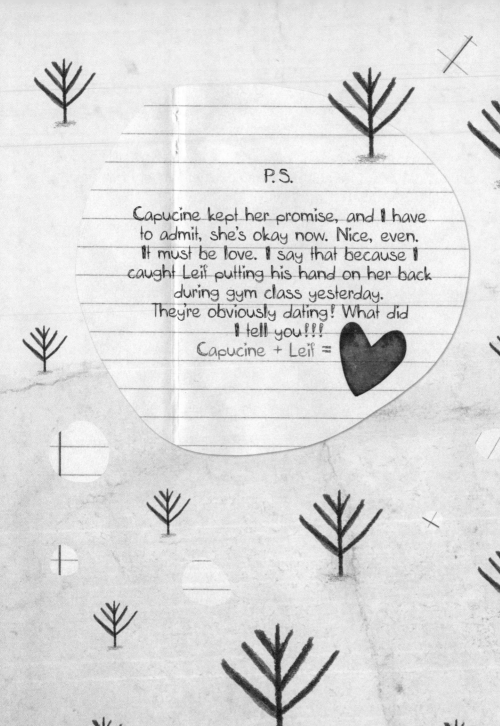

P.S.

Capucine kept her promise, and I have to admit, she's okay now. Nice, even. It must be love. I say that because I caught Leif putting his hand on her back during gym class yesterday. They're obviously dating! What did I tell you!!!

Capucine + Leif =

Orange juice, a deal, and a BIG DOSE OF COWARDICE

n black and white, ause everything in my head is gray right now.

"What are you doing, stink bug?"
"Nothing, just drawing."
"Can you come join us in the kitchen? We'd like to talk to you."
"Who's we?"
"Yoko and me."

When I walked into the kitchen this morning and saw Yoko dressed in these weird kimono-ish pajamas, it was pretty obvious she'd spent the night. It was also pretty obvious I basically had a stepmother now.

"Did she sleep over?"
"Franny! Ask Yoko if you really want to know. She's standing right here."

Yoko (who's starting to speak decent French, by the way) had understood every word:

"*Oui*, I sleep here. I hope is okay with you, Funny? If I . . ."
"Yeah, I don't mind. It's just . . . a little weird, because it's always been, well, just the two of us—me and Dad—but I don't mind, I promise."

Yoko got the gist of what I'd said, and I realized my father wasn't going to give me my orange juice until I sat down and listened to what he had to say.

So, I sat down.
Not like I had a choice.

"Dimitri is offering me a deal, sweetheart."
"I know, Sam told me. But he's completely insane if he thinks we're going to accept his money!"
" . . . "
"Dad? Why aren't you saying anything?"
" . . . "
"Tell me you're not thinking of accepting?!"
"It's really . . . a lot of money, Franny."
"So?!"

I stood up. Not like I had a choice.
I had a point to prove.

"Sweetheart, I'm touched you feel so strongly about all this, but it's a decision that doesn't really concern you . . ."
"Um, it totally concerns me that my father is too much of a coward to stand up for himself!"
"Franny! Don't speak to me like that! Not after everything I've been through!"
"I'll speak to you however I want!"
"That's enough! Go calm down, and when you're MATURE enough to have a rational discussion, I'll tell you what's going to happen next."
"Oh, because you've already decided, right?! As usual! I bet you've already bought the plane tickets and you're going to tell me I have 48 hours to pack my bags and say goodbye to my new friends?! I'll make new ones, right? No big deal! Is that it?"
"Franny."

"You know what, Dad? I will go to my room to calm down. But as for being immature, I don't think you're one to talk. So, don't even THINK about coming to apologize for being the most . . . ugh . . . Just forget about it!"

SERIOUSLY.

I had no words left
to express the inexpressible.
Me! At a loss for words. That doesn't happen every day.

P.S. //
I hope my father eventually comes back down
to earth and realizes
he's making the biggest mistake of his life.

Franny

Wednesday, May 17
(time irrelevant)

Still no mail

I'm writing only to tell you I still haven't gotten Henry's letter. Which isn't normal. It's been twelve days. And I'm almost out of pages, Diary. So sorry. I SWEAR I was planning to tell you everything, but right now, all I can do is think up ridiculous scenarios, like:

Did Henry write to me . . .

to declare his undying love for me?
to tell me to get out of his life forever?
to tell me he's met another . . . girl?

Eek

Honestly,
I haven't the faintest idea.

And it's not like I haven't been looking out for the letter: I've been to the post office so many times in the past few days that the clerk just shakes his head now, before I can even ask. And to think—if I'd only figured out what I wanted sooner . . . I wouldn't be in this situation now.

Crap.

I also wanted to tell you I've come to terms with the fact my father is going to accept the huge pile of cash Dimitri's offering him. Anyway, my father's always done whatever suited him, no matter what I thought, so what's the point in fighting it? The only mini catch: I have no idea how much money we're talking about, because my father CATEGORICALLY refuses to discuss it.

Oh.

It must be a lot if he's so intent on keeping it a secret, right? I mean, if it were just $20, he definitely would have told me. By the way, I think I'd make an excellent detective.

Wow.
So, does that mean we're, like, rich now?

Catch no. 2: My father spends ALL HIS TIME at home. Which is only normal since he doesn't have a job anymore. But weirdly enough, we're talking even less now than when he was trying to save the human race. By the way, I don't know what my father is cooking up, but if he's not telling me, it's probably because he knows I won't be cool with it. Don't you think, Diary?

BUT: GOOD NEWS!!!

Ms. Clara spoke to my father, and when he confirmed that everything we'd said was true, she offered to make an arrangement with us. Basically, she's giving us three extra weeks, and we can do our presentation in private (Sam was adamant the entire school not find out about his father, which I get). So, we're not going to fail social science after all!

Whew.
Yay, even.

Franny xxxx

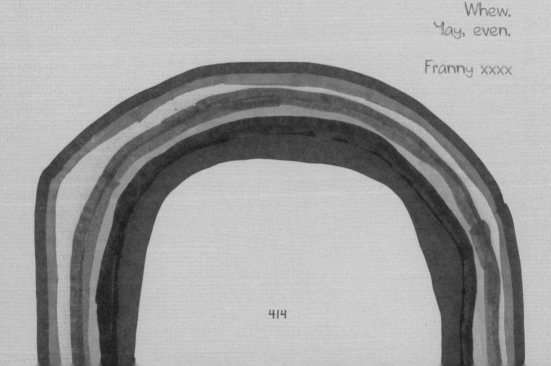

Train-ride decision

I have only three pages left, Diary, and I thought I'd save them for when I finally got Henry's letter, but I have no choice: I REALLY need to write to you.

I'm with Francine and old Manaka right now, on a train to Hiroshima. The bonsai that I (thankfully) didn't kill is officially healed, and the three of us are going to pick it up at the hospital, 125 miles away from Kyoto.

Francine is with us because I invited her to come along when she said she didn't believe there was such a thing as a bonsai hospital.

Funny that after living here for so many years, Francine still hasn't realized that ANYTHING IS POSSIBLE in Japan!

But it's a good thing.
I'm glad she's here.

I understand better—now that I'm on the train—why my father insisted on bringing us to the station this morning. For starters, as we were saying goodbye on the platform, he hugged me like it was the last time we'd ever see each other.

"We'll be back tomorrow, Dad. Tomorrow. Relax."

He handed me a letter. At the time, all I could think was . . . Oh no.

The last time he wrote me an actual letter, my life was turned COMPLETELY upside down.

"Read it on the train, sweetheart."

My father smiled at me, a sort of half apology for not having the guts to say what he had to say in person. When I realized he'd gone to the trouble of writing on beautiful Japanese stationery, I figured what he had to say must be kind of important.

"Dad, not so tight. You're suffocating me."
"Sorry. Okay, off you go. I love you."
"I love you too."
"And I'll love you no matter what you decide, stink bug."
"What do you mean? Decide what?"

Just as I was about to tell my father he wasn't going to get away with giving me some stupid letter and that I deserved a proper explanation, Manaka signaled to me: the train was about to leave.

With his fancy Japanese paper, my father had once again found a way to avoid a public confrontation.

I guess I don't really have a choice. I'll read his letter and then fill you in. Francine has already asked me to open it at least two hundred times!

Wish me luck, Diary. xx

Dear Franny,

I thought I should write you this letter since we've had so many misunderstandings lately. I hope it's not the wrong move. I've always found trains to be the best places for thinking. Don't you agree?

I know I've pretty much done everything my way since the minute I won that contest. And I know I became completely obsessed with my research. With the thought of doing something great, something important. I became swept up by it all, and, ironically, you're the one who helped me see things clearly.

But in the meantime, I know I shut you out of all the decisions we had to make. And that's not what a family does. Not our family, anyway. So, I'm writing to tell you about my latest and greatest idea! I know you're going to love it! At least, I hope so . . . (?) I won't beat around the bush, so here goes: this time, sweetheart, YOU get to decide for our family. That's right, stink bug, it's up to YOU where we go next!!!!

So, we have two OPTIONS (exciting, right?).

PLAN A: Africa. Yes, you read that right! AFRICA! Yoko's been offered a job with an organization in Cameroon that protects large primates. We could go together, all three of us, and I even have a brilliant idea for you!!!

PLAN B: I've found a little house for sale, in St. Lorette. I know you liked it there. Maybe we could . . . move there? The house is old, but it would only be temporary. A test run.

What do you say? Your old pops is pretty cool, eh? All right, so you take all the time you need to think about it, stink bug (but not too long!). It's YOUR DECISION. The WORLD is your oyster!!! I'll take care of all the rest, I promise!

One click, two (or 3) plane tickets . . . and we're on our way!

I love you,
DAD xxxxxx

SERIOUSLY.

No, but, seriously.
How does he do
that?

I mean, I was sure—absolutely sure—my father had exhausted every possible and imaginable way of surprising me. But no.

Once again, he's
outdone himself.

And how am I supposed to know what to decide? I couldn't even find Cameroon on a map! I need to talk to Leona. OMG. I just had an idea. Oh!!!! An amazing idea!!!

But I'm out
of pages...

CRAP

CRAP

CRAP

Okay. I'm making you an unbreakable PROMISE. I won't tell my father what I decide until he buys me a new diary. I have no idea what the next few months have in store for me, but I know one thing for sure: you'll be with me every step of the way.

To be continued. Really, really soon!
Whew.

Franny xx

© Dominique Laurence

Stéphanie Lapointe

Stéphanie is a jack-of-all-trades who wears many hats. She feels happiest when she's recording an album, playing piano, or acting in a movie. While flying isn't high on her list of favorite things to do, now and then she'll get on a plane to film a documentary: her projects have taken her to Peru, Rwanda, Sudan, Mali, and Haiti.

After a nudge from one of her friends (who's not one to mince words), Stéphanie ventured into the world of writing. She was still in bed, one morning in November 2016, when she got the news that her book *Grandfather and the Moon* had won a Governor General's Literary Award.

Today, Stéphanie lives in Montreal in a pink-and-white house she built with someone she loves. Her favorite thing to do is lounge around all morning in her PJs, turn on her computer, and dream up stories.

Ann Marie Boulanger

Ann Marie is a translator, a teacher, and a trainer who was raised in the picturesque town of Rawdon, Quebec, Canada. She grew up speaking both English and French.

She owns a boutique translation firm, and when she's not translating serious documents about serious things, she loves to translate books—picture books and fairy tales for kids, and novels and short stories for adults. Her translation *The Woman in Valencia*, by Annie Perreault, was named a Notable Translation of 2021 by *World Literature Today*.

Ann Marie loves to read and write (she actually kept a diary herself for many years). She is now happily settled in Montreal, with her young son, doing work she adores surrounded by family and friends.

W1-Media, Inc.
Arctis Books USA
Stamford, CT, USA

Copyright © 2024 by W1-Media Inc. for this edition
First edition published in Canada under the title: *Fanny Cloutier ou L'année où mon père
m'a forcée à le suivre au bout du bout du monde, tome 2* © les éditions Les Malins, 2018
First hardcover English edition published by W1-Media Inc. / Arctis Books USA 2024

Visit our website at www.arctis-books.com

1 3 5 7 9 8 6 4 2

The Library of Congress Control Number: 2023940279

ISBN 978-1-64690-025-1
English translation copyright © Ann Marie Boulanger, 2024

Cover and interior illustrations by Marianne Ferrer
Printed in China

MIX
Paper | Supporting
responsible forestry
FSC
www.fsc.org   FSC® C020056